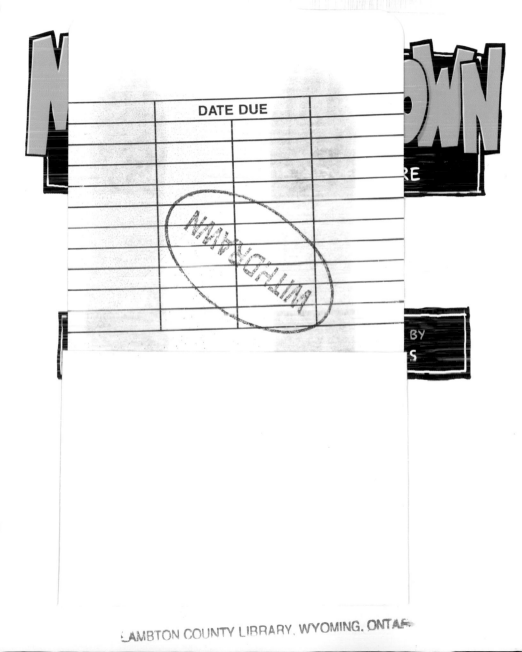

DATE DUE		

For Melanie, social media connoisseur, critic and l33t haxx0r.
Thanks to Antonio Lopez for his media literacy wisdom and ad hook insight. —LOD

Thanks to the family for the years of support.
Mom, Pops, Adam, Sarah, D.J., Kaylee, Justin and Nancy. —MD

Text copyright © 2009 Liam O'Donnell
Illustrations copyright © 2009 Mike Deas

Library and Archives Canada Cataloguing in Publication

O'Donnell, Liam, 1970-
Media meltdown : a graphic guide adventure / written by
Liam O'Donnell ; illustrated by Mike Deas.

c 2.   ISBN 978-1-55469-065-7

1. Media literacy--Comic books, strips, etc.--Juvenile fiction.

I. Deas, Mike, 1982- II. Title.

PS8579.D649R42 2001   j741.5'971   C2009-902580-9

First published in the United States, 2009

Library of Congress Control Number: 2009927573

Summary: While learning about media consolidation and the power of money over truth, Bounce, Pema and
Jagroop decide to take on greedy developers and the media they control, in graphic novel format.

Orca Book Publishers gratefully acknowledges the support for its publishing programs provided by the
following agencies: the Government of Canada through the Book Publishing Industry Development
Program and the Canada Council for the Arts, and the Province of British Columbia through the BC Arts
Council and the Book Publishing Tax Credit.

Cover and interior artwork by Mike Deas
Cover layout by Teresa Bubela
Author photo by Melanie McBride • Illustrator photo by Ellen Ho

ORCA BOOK PUBLISHERS   ORCA BOOK PUBLISHERS
PO Box 5626, STN. B   PO Box 468
VICTORIA, BC CANADA   CUSTER, WA USA
V8R 6S4   98240-0468

www.orcabook.com
Printed and bound in China.
12 11 10 09 • 4 3 2 1

CHAPTER 1

BEHIND THE NEWS

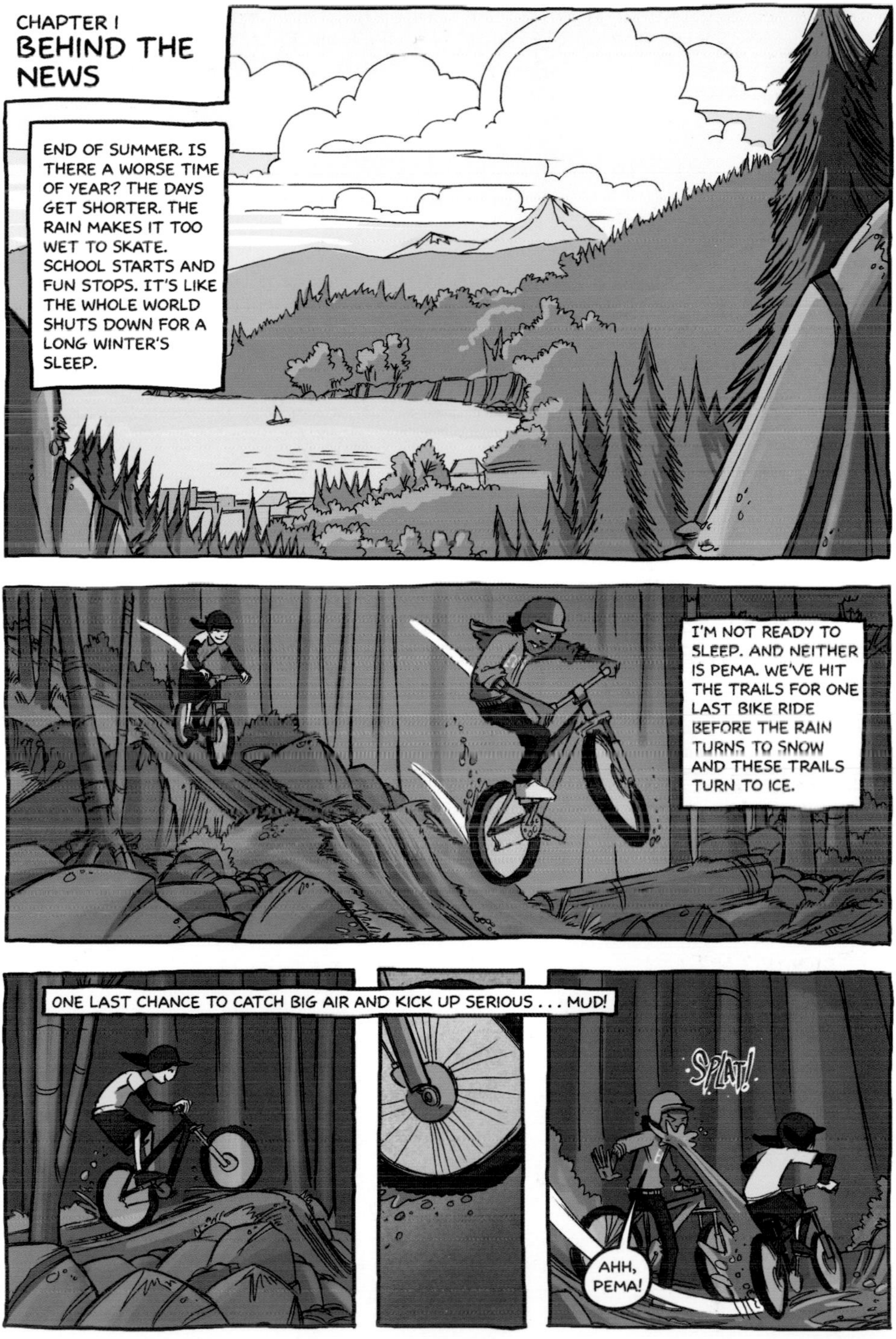

END OF SUMMER. IS THERE A WORSE TIME OF YEAR? THE DAYS GET SHORTER. THE RAIN MAKES IT TOO WET TO SKATE. SCHOOL STARTS AND FUN STOPS. IT'S LIKE THE WHOLE WORLD SHUTS DOWN FOR A LONG WINTER'S SLEEP.
I'M NOT READY TO SLEEP. AND NEITHER IS PEMA. WE'VE HIT THE TRAILS FOR ONE LAST BIKE RIDE BEFORE THE RAIN TURNS TO SNOW AND THESE TRAILS TURN TO ICE.
ONE LAST CHANCE TO CATCH BIG AIR AND KICK UP SERIOUS . . . MUD!
SPLAT!
AHH, PEMA!

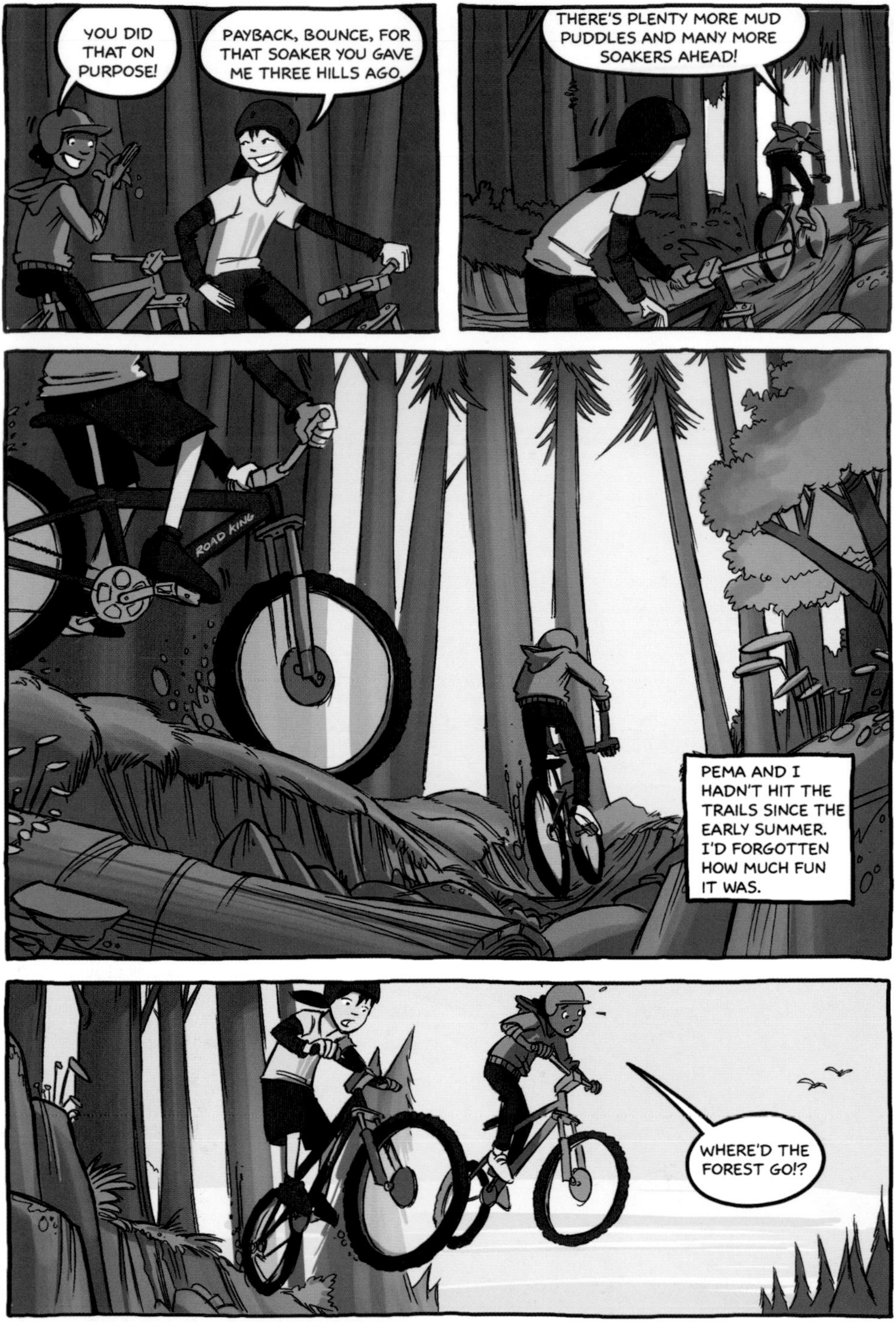
YOU DID THAT ON PURPOSE!
PAYBACK, BOUNCE, FOR THAT SOAKER YOU GAVE ME THREE HILLS AGO.
THERE'S PLENTY MORE MUD PUDDLES AND MANY MORE SOAKERS AHEAD!
ROAD KING
PEMA AND I HADN'T HIT THE TRAILS SINCE THE EARLY SUMMER. I'D FORGOTTEN HOW MUCH FUN IT WAS.
WHERE'D THE FOREST GO!?

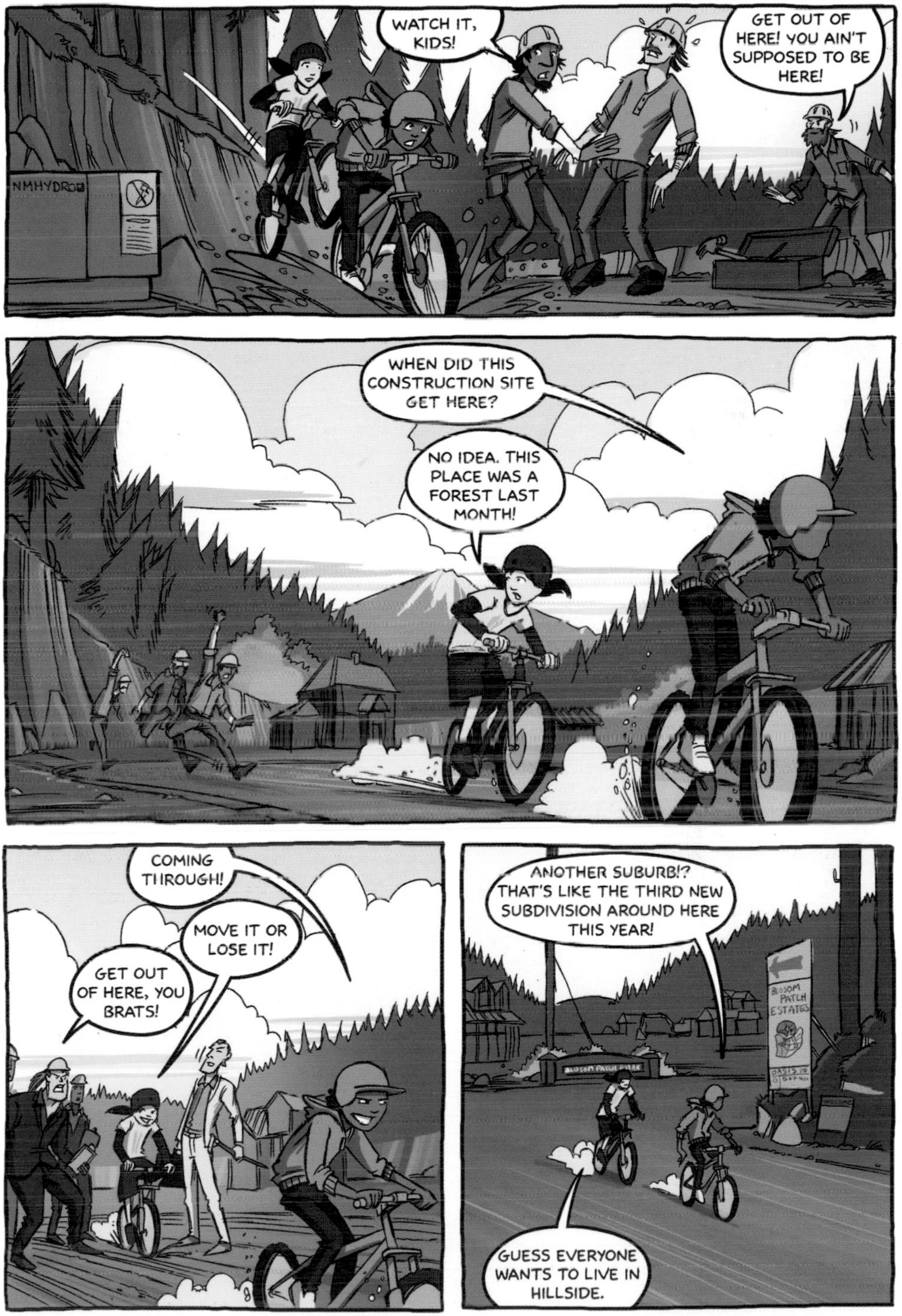
WATCH IT, KIDS!
NMHYDRO
GET OUT OF HERE! YOU AIN'T SUPPOSED TO BE HERE!
WHEN DID THIS CONSTRUCTION SITE GET HERE?
NO IDEA. THIS PLACE WAS A FOREST LAST MONTH!
COMING THROUGH!
MOVE IT OR LOSE IT!
GET OUT OF HERE, YOU BRATS!
ANOTHER SUBURB!? THAT'S LIKE THE THIRD NEW SUBDIVISION AROUND HERE THIS YEAR!
BLOSOM PATCH ESTATES
GUESS EVERYONE WANTS TO LIVE IN HILLSIDE.

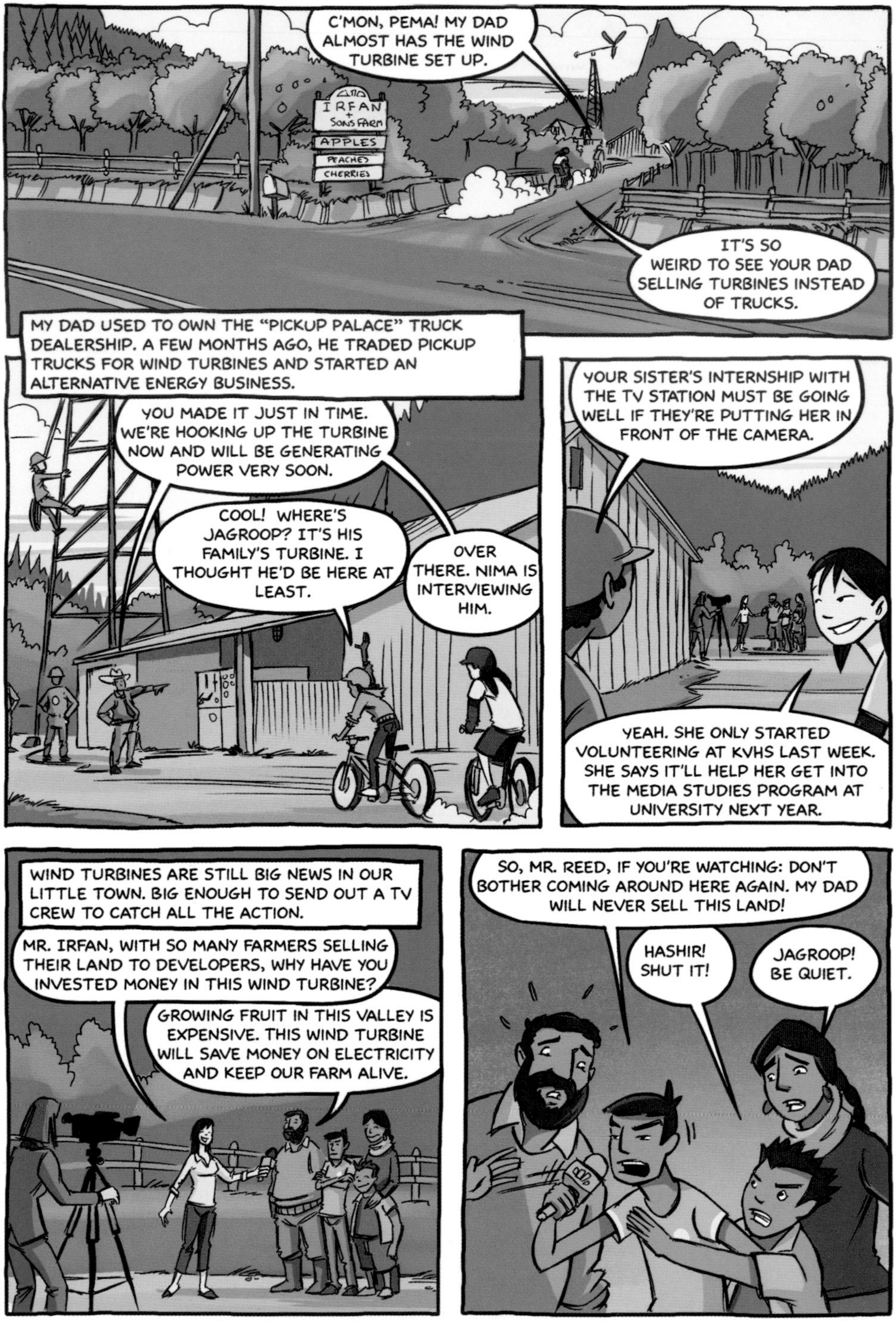
C'MON, PEMA! MY DAD ALMOST HAS THE WIND TURBINE SET UP.
IRFAN + SONS FARM
APPLES
PEACHES
CHERRIES
IT'S SO WEIRD TO SEE YOUR DAD SELLING TURBINES INSTEAD OF TRUCKS.
MY DAD USED TO OWN THE "PICKUP PALACE" TRUCK DEALERSHIP. A FEW MONTHS AGO, HE TRADED PICKUP TRUCKS FOR WIND TURBINES AND STARTED AN ALTERNATIVE ENERGY BUSINESS.
YOU MADE IT JUST IN TIME. WE'RE HOOKING UP THE TURBINE NOW AND WILL BE GENERATING POWER VERY SOON.
COOL! WHERE'S JAGROOP? IT'S HIS FAMILY'S TURBINE. I THOUGHT HE'D BE HERE AT LEAST.
OVER THERE. NIMA IS INTERVIEWING HIM.
YOUR SISTER'S INTERNSHIP WITH THE TV STATION MUST BE GOING WELL IF THEY'RE PUTTING HER IN FRONT OF THE CAMERA.
YEAH. SHE ONLY STARTED VOLUNTEERING AT KVHS LAST WEEK. SHE SAYS IT'LL HELP HER GET INTO THE MEDIA STUDIES PROGRAM AT UNIVERSITY NEXT YEAR.
WIND TURBINES ARE STILL BIG NEWS IN OUR LITTLE TOWN. BIG ENOUGH TO SEND OUT A TV CREW TO CATCH ALL THE ACTION.
MR. IRFAN, WITH SO MANY FARMERS SELLING THEIR LAND TO DEVELOPERS, WHY HAVE YOU INVESTED MONEY IN THIS WIND TURBINE?
GROWING FRUIT IN THIS VALLEY IS EXPENSIVE. THIS WIND TURBINE WILL SAVE MONEY ON ELECTRICITY AND KEEP OUR FARM ALIVE.
SO, MR. REED, IF YOU'RE WATCHING: DON'T BOTHER COMING AROUND HERE AGAIN. MY DAD WILL NEVER SELL THIS LAND!
HASHIR! SHUT IT!
JAGROOP! BE QUIET.

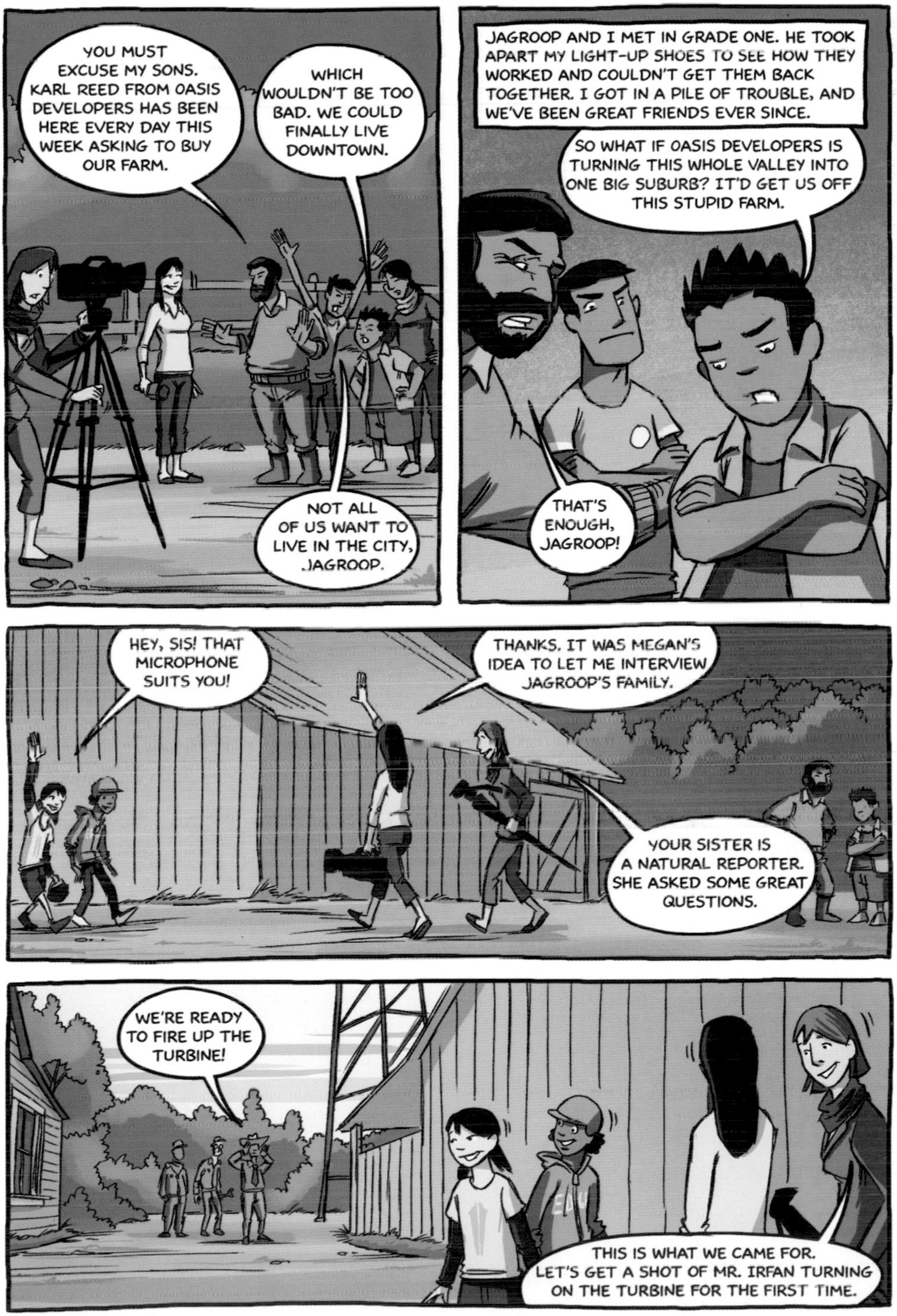
YOU MUST EXCUSE MY SONS. KARL REED FROM OASIS DEVELOPERS HAS BEEN HERE EVERY DAY THIS WEEK ASKING TO BUY OUR FARM.
WHICH WOULDN'T BE TOO BAD. WE COULD FINALLY LIVE DOWNTOWN.
NOT ALL OF US WANT TO LIVE IN THE CITY, JAGROOP.
JAGROOP AND I MET IN GRADE ONE. HE TOOK APART MY LIGHT-UP SHOES TO SEE HOW THEY WORKED AND COULDN'T GET THEM BACK TOGETHER. I GOT IN A PILE OF TROUBLE, AND WE'VE BEEN GREAT FRIENDS EVER SINCE.
SO WHAT IF OASIS DEVELOPERS IS TURNING THIS WHOLE VALLEY INTO ONE BIG SUBURB? IT'D GET US OFF THIS STUPID FARM.
THAT'S ENOUGH, JAGROOP!
HEY, SIS! THAT MICROPHONE SUITS YOU!
THANKS. IT WAS MEGAN'S IDEA TO LET ME INTERVIEW JAGROOP'S FAMILY.
YOUR SISTER IS A NATURAL REPORTER. SHE ASKED SOME GREAT QUESTIONS.
WE'RE READY TO FIRE UP THE TURBINE!
THIS IS WHAT WE CAME FOR. LET'S GET A SHOT OF MR. IRFAN TURNING ON THE TURBINE FOR THE FIRST TIME.

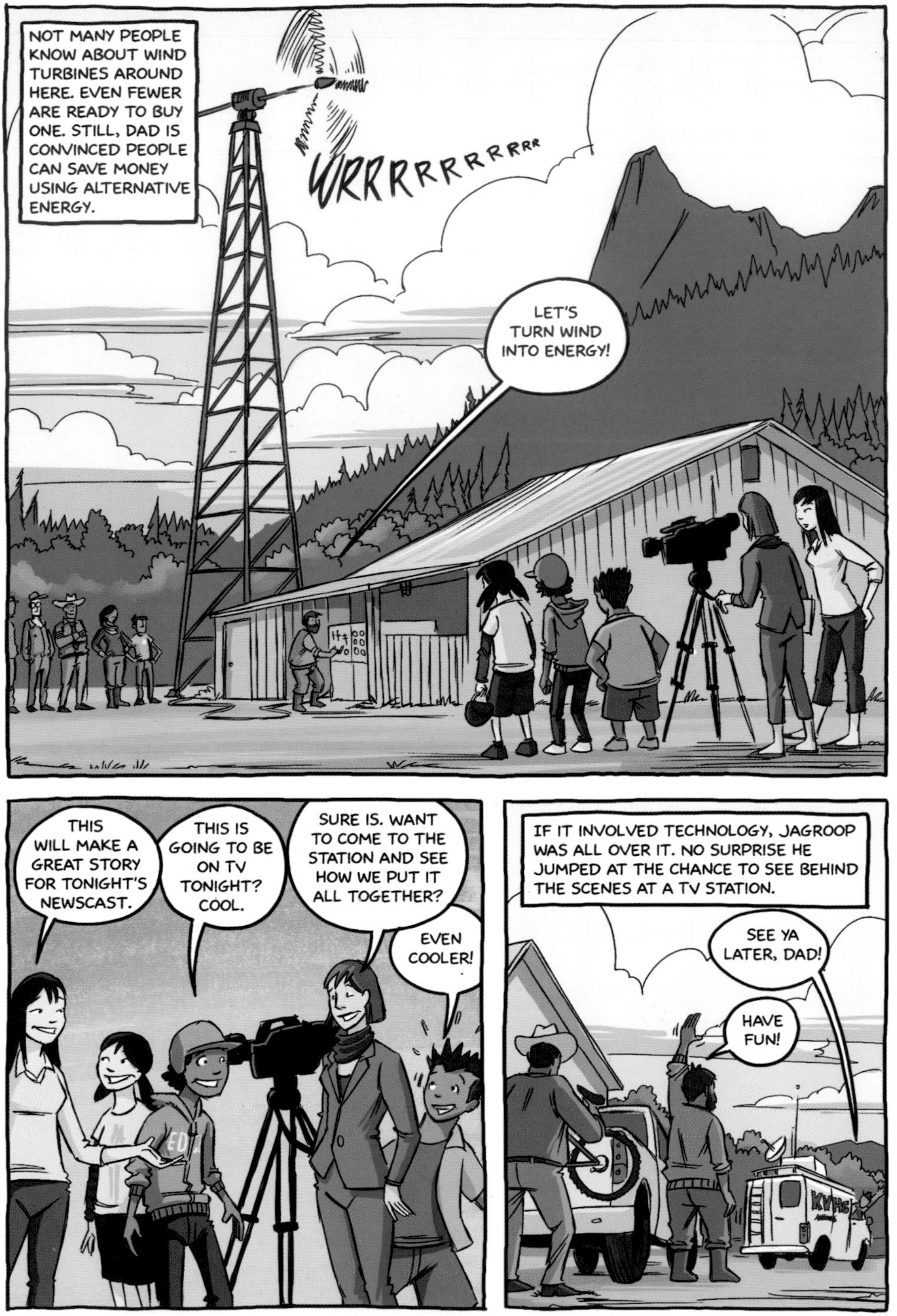
NOT MANY PEOPLE KNOW ABOUT WIND TURBINES AROUND HERE. EVEN FEWER ARE READY TO BUY ONE. STILL, DAD IS CONVINCED PEOPLE CAN SAVE MONEY USING ALTERNATIVE ENERGY.
WRRRRRRRRRR
LET'S TURN WIND INTO ENERGY!
THIS WILL MAKE A GREAT STORY FOR TONIGHT'S NEWSCAST.
THIS IS GOING TO BE ON TV TONIGHT? COOL.
SURE IS. WANT TO COME TO THE STATION AND SEE HOW WE PUT IT ALL TOGETHER?
EVEN COOLER!
IF IT INVOLVED TECHNOLOGY, JAGROOP WAS ALL OVER IT. NO SURPRISE HE JUMPED AT THE CHANCE TO SEE BEHIND THE SCENES AT A TV STATION.
SEE YA LATER, DAD!
HAVE FUN!

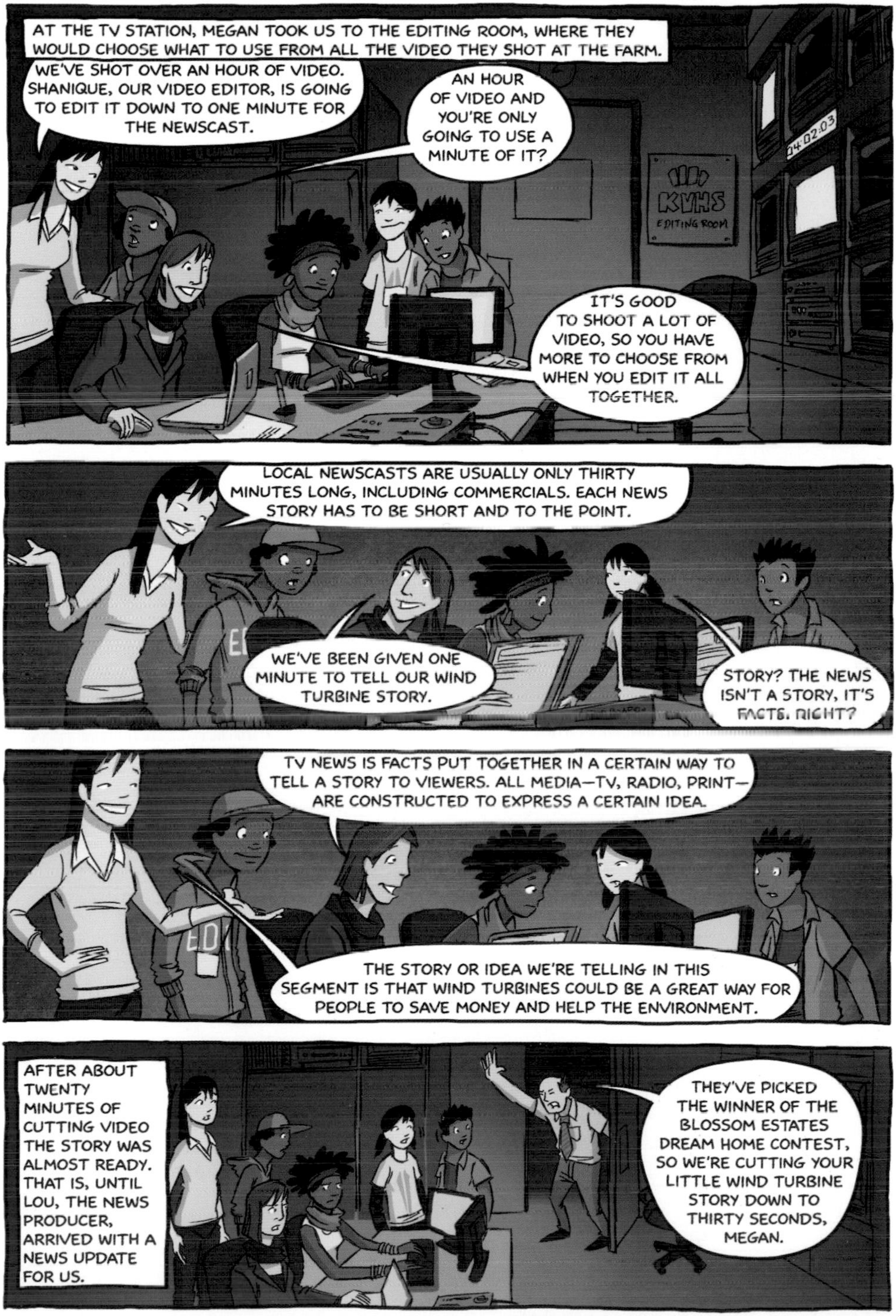
AT THE TV STATION, MEGAN TOOK US TO THE EDITING ROOM, WHERE THEY WOULD CHOOSE WHAT TO USE FROM ALL THE VIDEO THEY SHOT AT THE FARM.
WE'VE SHOT OVER AN HOUR OF VIDEO. SHANIQUE, OUR VIDEO EDITOR, IS GOING TO EDIT IT DOWN TO ONE MINUTE FOR THE NEWSCAST.
AN HOUR OF VIDEO AND YOU'RE ONLY GOING TO USE A MINUTE OF IT?
KVHS
EDITING ROOM
04:02:03
IT'S GOOD TO SHOOT A LOT OF VIDEO, SO YOU HAVE MORE TO CHOOSE FROM WHEN YOU EDIT IT ALL TOGETHER.
LOCAL NEWSCASTS ARE USUALLY ONLY THIRTY MINUTES LONG, INCLUDING COMMERCIALS. EACH NEWS STORY HAS TO BE SHORT AND TO THE POINT.
WE'VE BEEN GIVEN ONE MINUTE TO TELL OUR WIND TURBINE STORY.
STORY? THE NEWS ISN'T A STORY, IT'S FACTS, RIGHT?
TV NEWS IS FACTS PUT TOGETHER IN A CERTAIN WAY TO TELL A STORY TO VIEWERS. ALL MEDIA—TV, RADIO, PRINT—ARE CONSTRUCTED TO EXPRESS A CERTAIN IDEA.
THE STORY OR IDEA WE'RE TELLING IN THIS SEGMENT IS THAT WIND TURBINES COULD BE A GREAT WAY FOR PEOPLE TO SAVE MONEY AND HELP THE ENVIRONMENT.
AFTER ABOUT TWENTY MINUTES OF CUTTING VIDEO THE STORY WAS ALMOST READY. THAT IS, UNTIL LOU, THE NEWS PRODUCER, ARRIVED WITH A NEWS UPDATE FOR US.
THEY'VE PICKED THE WINNER OF THE BLOSSOM ESTATES DREAM HOME CONTEST, SO WE'RE CUTTING YOUR LITTLE WIND TURBINE STORY DOWN TO THIRTY SECONDS, MEGAN.

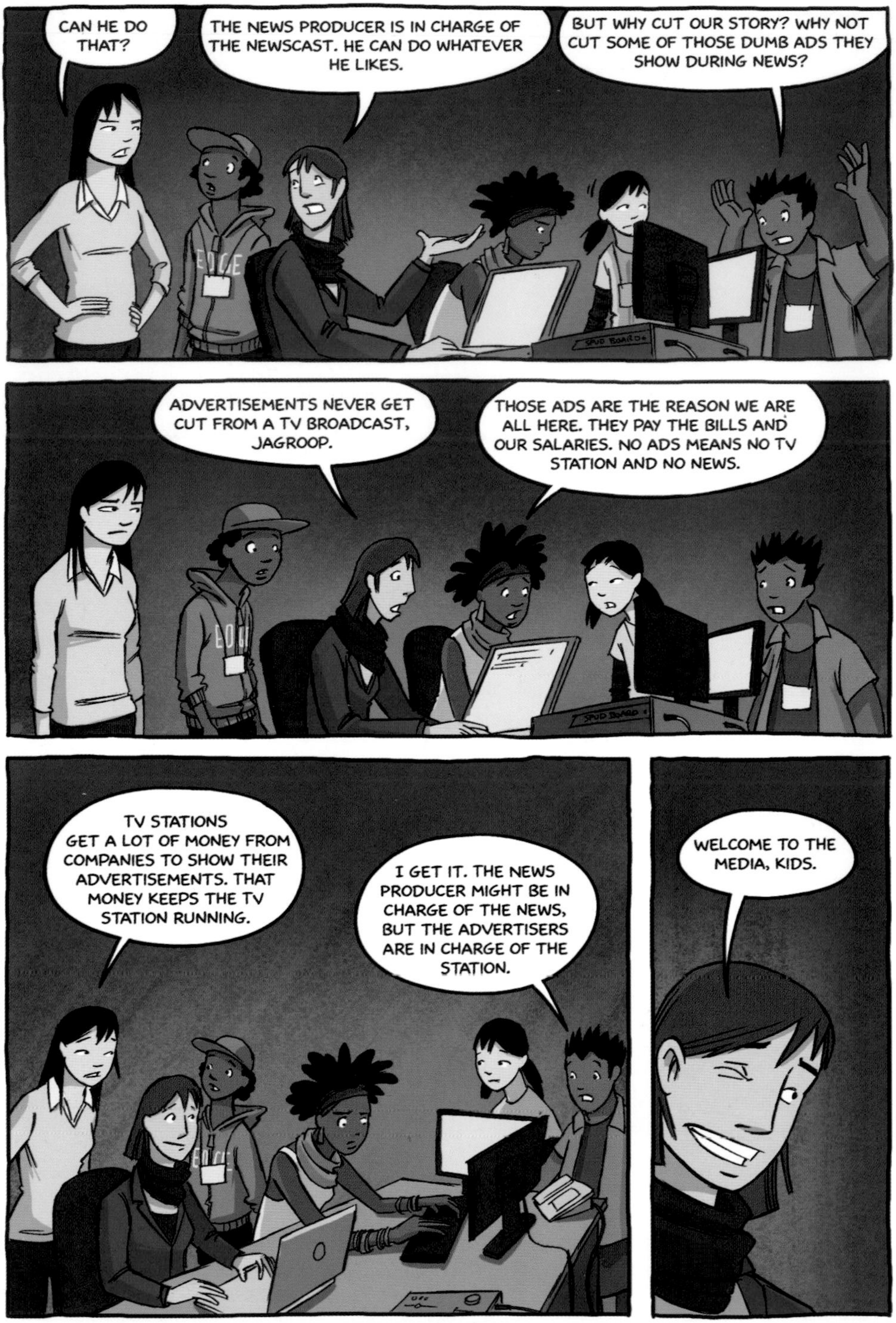
CAN HE DO THAT?
THE NEWS PRODUCER IS IN CHARGE OF THE NEWSCAST. HE CAN DO WHATEVER HE LIKES.
BUT WHY CUT OUR STORY? WHY NOT CUT SOME OF THOSE DUMB ADS THEY SHOW DURING NEWS?
EDGE
SPUD BOARD
ADVERTISEMENTS NEVER GET CUT FROM A TV BROADCAST, JAGROOP.
THOSE ADS ARE THE REASON WE ARE ALL HERE. THEY PAY THE BILLS AND OUR SALARIES. NO ADS MEANS NO TV STATION AND NO NEWS.
TV STATIONS GET A LOT OF MONEY FROM COMPANIES TO SHOW THEIR ADVERTISEMENTS. THAT MONEY KEEPS THE TV STATION RUNNING.
I GET IT. THE NEWS PRODUCER MIGHT BE IN CHARGE OF THE NEWS, BUT THE ADVERTISERS ARE IN CHARGE OF THE STATION.
WELCOME TO THE MEDIA, KIDS.

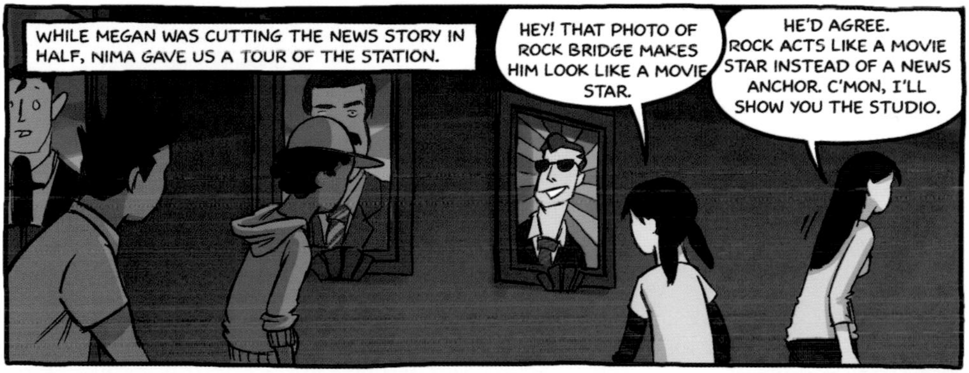
WHILE MEGAN WAS CUTTING THE NEWS STORY IN HALF, NIMA GAVE US A TOUR OF THE STATION.
HEY! THAT PHOTO OF ROCK BRIDGE MAKES HIM LOOK LIKE A MOVIE STAR.
HE'D AGREE. ROCK ACTS LIKE A MOVIE STAR INSTEAD OF A NEWS ANCHOR. C'MON, I'LL SHOW YOU THE STUDIO.

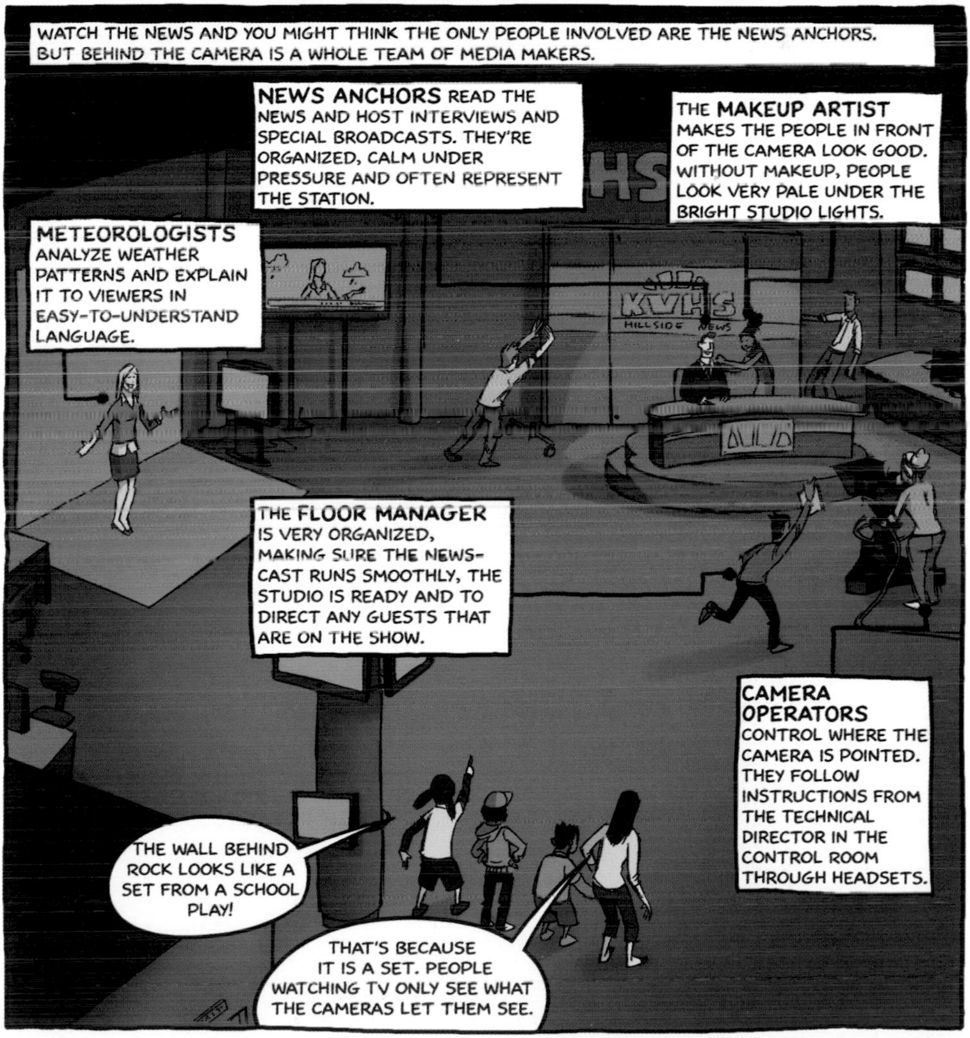
WATCH THE NEWS AND YOU MIGHT THINK THE ONLY PEOPLE INVOLVED ARE THE NEWS ANCHORS. BUT BEHIND THE CAMERA IS A WHOLE TEAM OF MEDIA MAKERS.
NEWS ANCHORS READ THE NEWS AND HOST INTERVIEWS AND SPECIAL BROADCASTS. THEY'RE ORGANIZED, CALM UNDER PRESSURE AND OFTEN REPRESENT THE STATION.
THE MAKEUP ARTIST MAKES THE PEOPLE IN FRONT OF THE CAMERA LOOK GOOD. WITHOUT MAKEUP, PEOPLE LOOK VERY PALE UNDER THE BRIGHT STUDIO LIGHTS.
METEOROLOGISTS ANALYZE WEATHER PATTERNS AND EXPLAIN IT TO VIEWERS IN EASY-TO-UNDERSTAND LANGUAGE.
KVHS
HILLSIDE NEWS
THE FLOOR MANAGER IS VERY ORGANIZED, MAKING SURE THE NEWS-CAST RUNS SMOOTHLY, THE STUDIO IS READY AND TO DIRECT ANY GUESTS THAT ARE ON THE SHOW.
CAMERA OPERATORS CONTROL WHERE THE CAMERA IS POINTED. THEY FOLLOW INSTRUCTIONS FROM THE TECHNICAL DIRECTOR IN THE CONTROL ROOM THROUGH HEADSETS.
THE WALL BEHIND ROCK LOOKS LIKE A SET FROM A SCHOOL PLAY!
THAT'S BECAUSE IT IS A SET. PEOPLE WATCHING TV ONLY SEE WHAT THE CAMERAS LET THEM SEE.

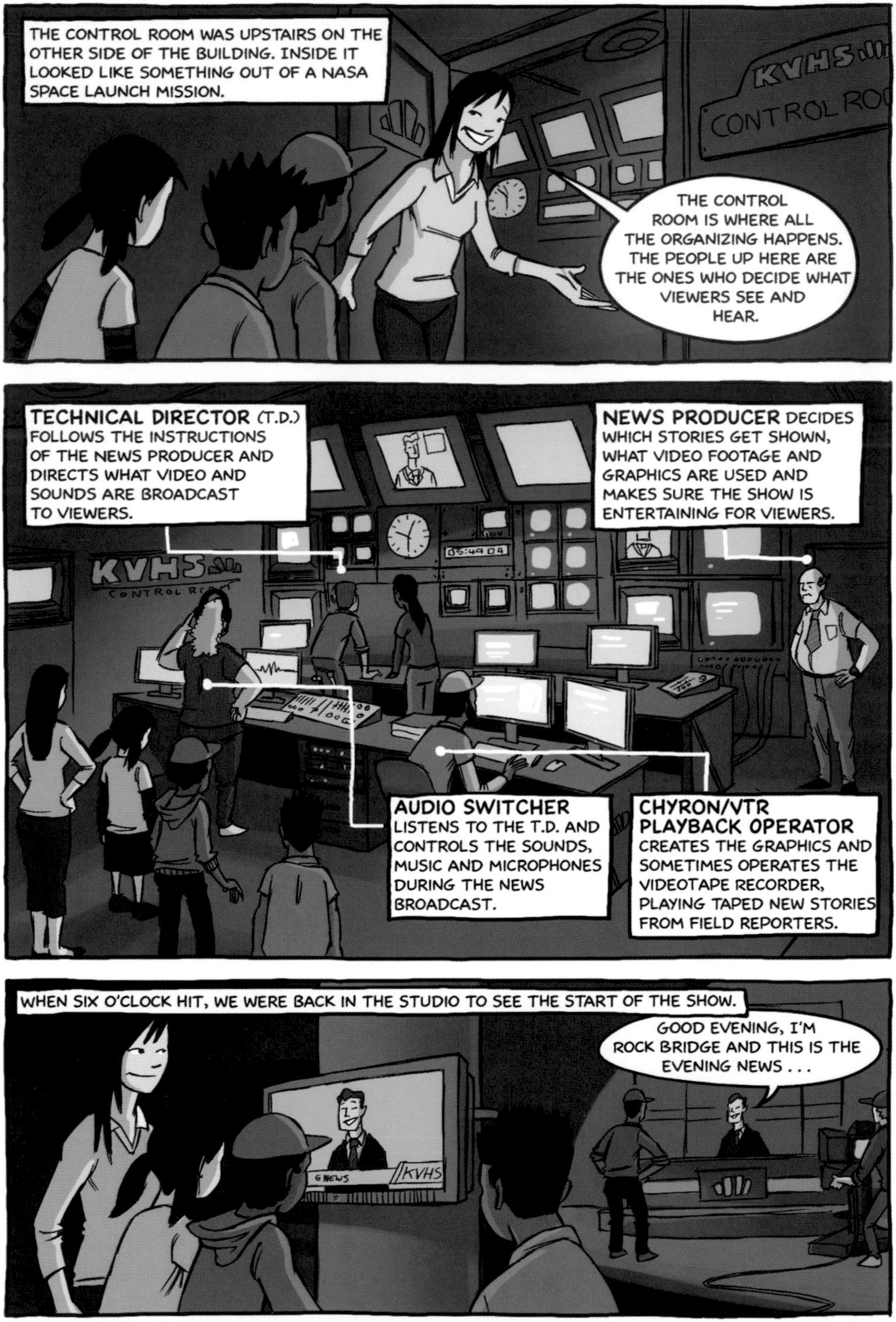
THE CONTROL ROOM WAS UPSTAIRS ON THE OTHER SIDE OF THE BUILDING. INSIDE IT LOOKED LIKE SOMETHING OUT OF A NASA SPACE LAUNCH MISSION.
KVHS
CONTROL RO
THE CONTROL ROOM IS WHERE ALL THE ORGANIZING HAPPENS. THE PEOPLE UP HERE ARE THE ONES WHO DECIDE WHAT VIEWERS SEE AND HEAR.
TECHNICAL DIRECTOR (T.D.) FOLLOWS THE INSTRUCTIONS OF THE NEWS PRODUCER AND DIRECTS WHAT VIDEO AND SOUNDS ARE BROADCAST TO VIEWERS.
NEWS PRODUCER DECIDES WHICH STORIES GET SHOWN, WHAT VIDEO FOOTAGE AND GRAPHICS ARE USED AND MAKES SURE THE SHOW IS ENTERTAINING FOR VIEWERS.
05:49 04
KVHS
AUDIO SWITCHER LISTENS TO THE T.D. AND CONTROLS THE SOUNDS, MUSIC AND MICROPHONES DURING THE NEWS BROADCAST.
CHYRON/VTR PLAYBACK OPERATOR CREATES THE GRAPHICS AND SOMETIMES OPERATES THE VIDEOTAPE RECORDER, PLAYING TAPED NEW STORIES FROM FIELD REPORTERS.
WHEN SIX O'CLOCK HIT, WE WERE BACK IN THE STUDIO TO SEE THE START OF THE SHOW.
GOOD EVENING, I'M ROCK BRIDGE AND THIS IS THE EVENING NEWS . . .
6 NEWS
KVHS

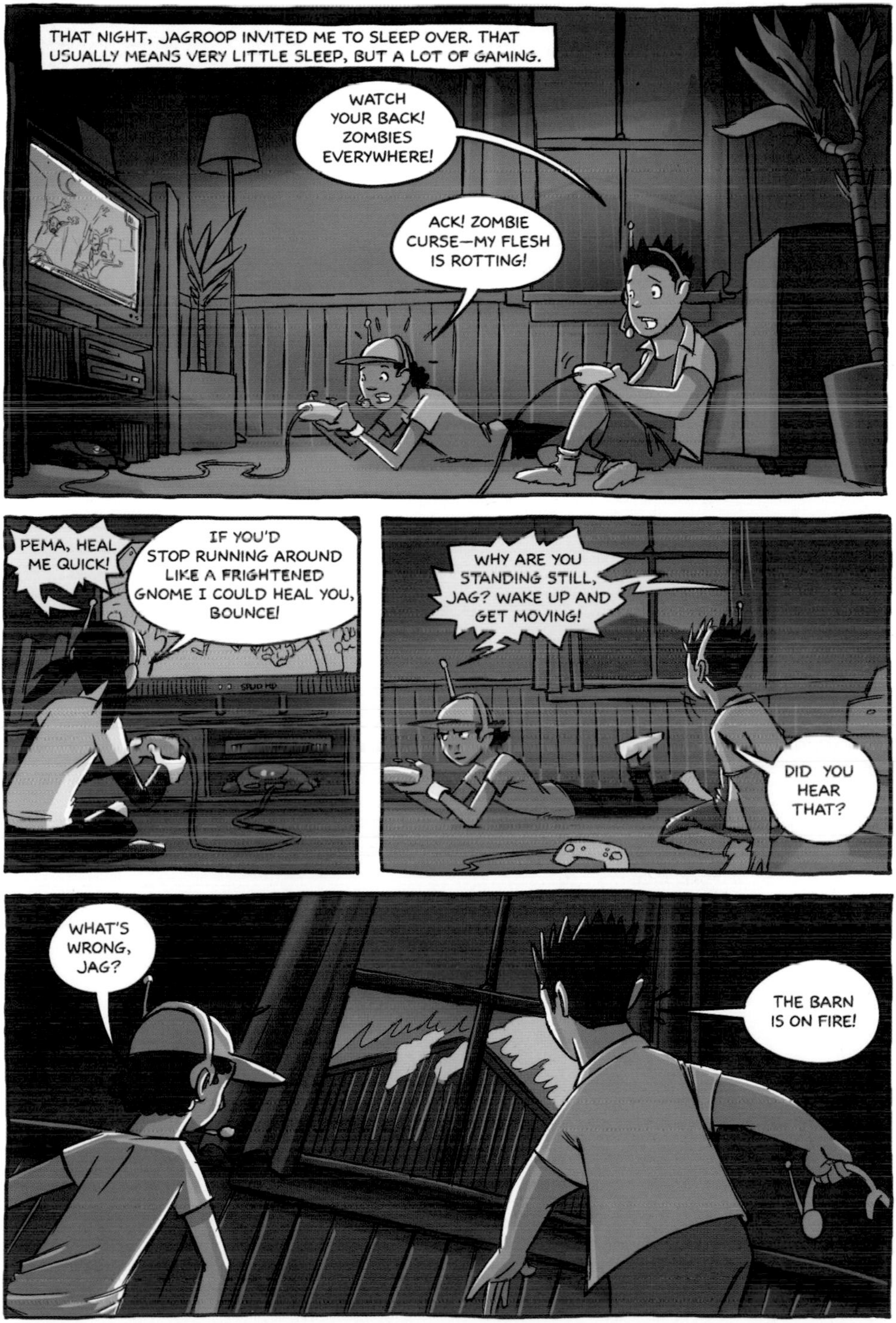
THAT NIGHT, JAGROOP INVITED ME TO SLEEP OVER. THAT USUALLY MEANS VERY LITTLE SLEEP, BUT A LOT OF GAMING.
WATCH YOUR BACK! ZOMBIES EVERYWHERE!
ACK! ZOMBIE CURSE—MY FLESH IS ROTTING!
PEMA, HEAL ME QUICK!
IF YOU'D STOP RUNNING AROUND LIKE A FRIGHTENED GNOME I COULD HEAL YOU, BOUNCE!
WHY ARE YOU STANDING STILL, JAG? WAKE UP AND GET MOVING!
DID YOU HEAR THAT?
WHAT'S WRONG, JAG?
THE BARN IS ON FIRE!

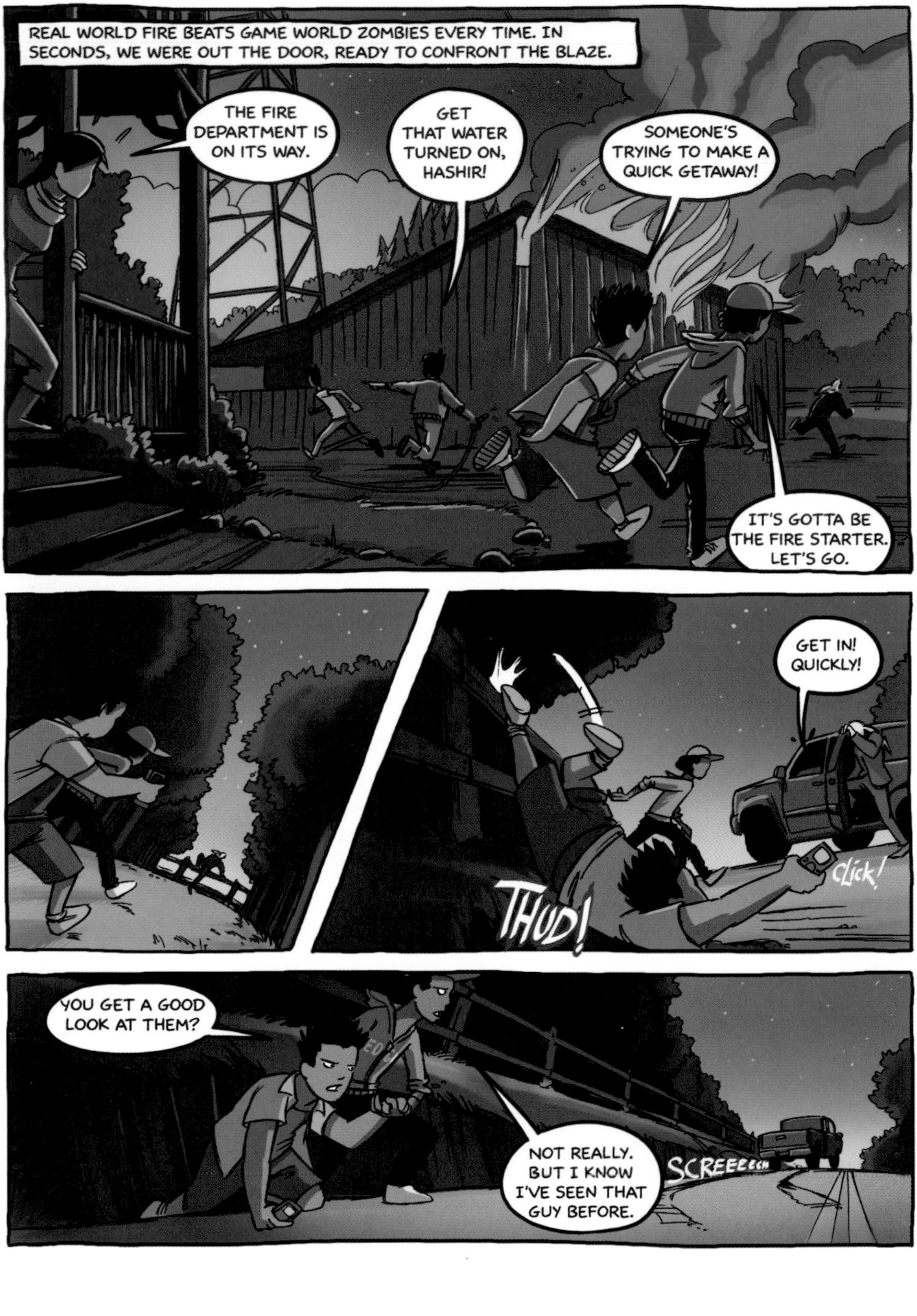
REAL WORLD FIRE BEATS GAME WORLD ZOMBIES EVERY TIME. IN SECONDS, WE WERE OUT THE DOOR, READY TO CONFRONT THE BLAZE.
THE FIRE DEPARTMENT IS ON ITS WAY.
GET THAT WATER TURNED ON, HASHIR!
SOMEONE'S TRYING TO MAKE A QUICK GETAWAY!
IT'S GOTTA BE THE FIRE STARTER. LET'S GO.
GET IN! QUICKLY!
CLICK!
THUD!
YOU GET A GOOD LOOK AT THEM?
NOT REALLY. BUT I KNOW I'VE SEEN THAT GUY BEFORE.
SCREEEECH

CHAPTER 2
CUTTING THE TRUTH

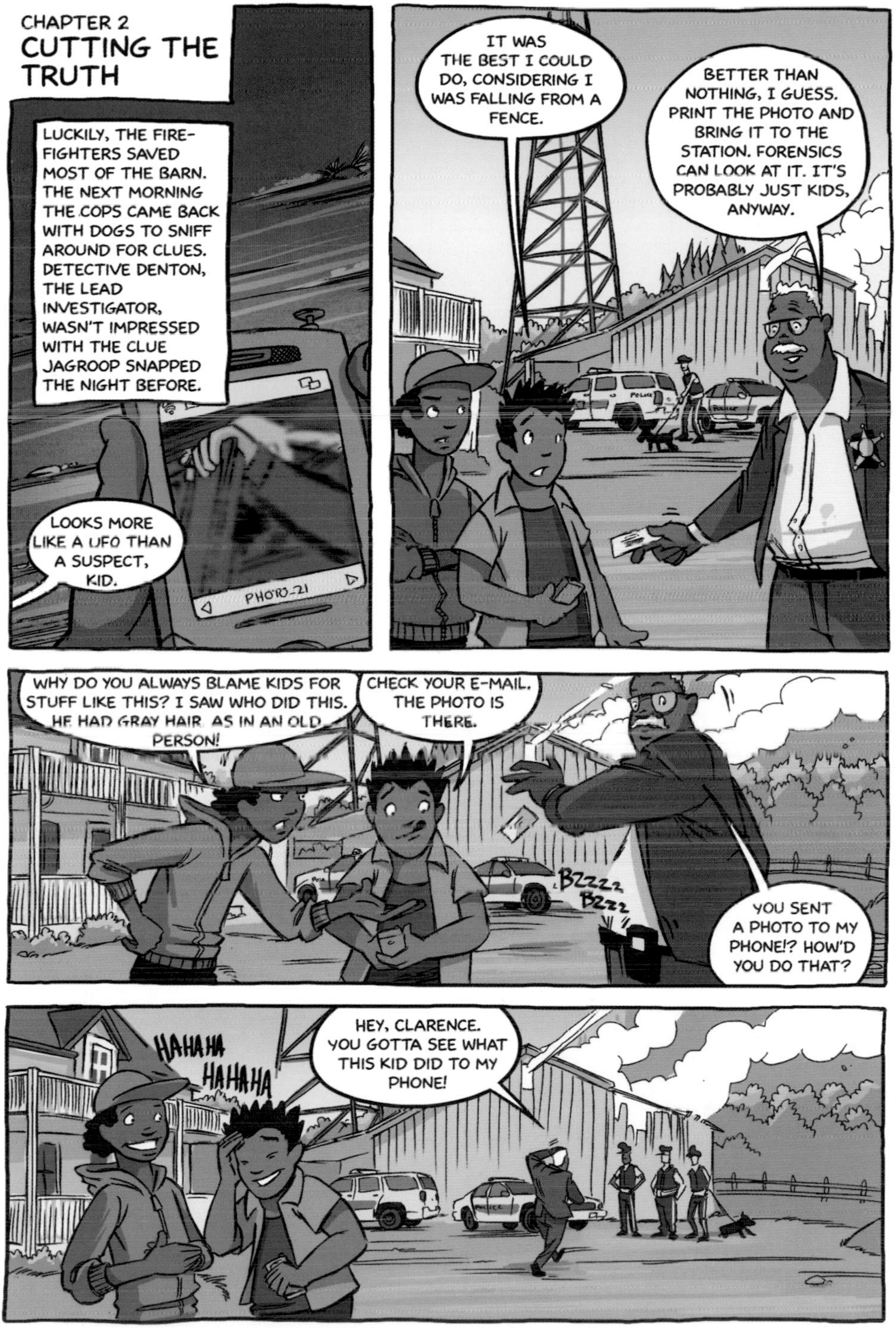

LUCKILY, THE FIRE-FIGHTERS SAVED MOST OF THE BARN. THE NEXT MORNING THE COPS CAME BACK WITH DOGS TO SNIFF AROUND FOR CLUES. DETECTIVE DENTON, THE LEAD INVESTIGATOR, WASN'T IMPRESSED WITH THE CLUE JAGROOP SNAPPED THE NIGHT BEFORE.
PHOTO_21
LOOKS MORE LIKE A UFO THAN A SUSPECT, KID.
IT WAS THE BEST I COULD DO, CONSIDERING I WAS FALLING FROM A FENCE.
BETTER THAN NOTHING, I GUESS. PRINT THE PHOTO AND BRING IT TO THE STATION. FORENSICS CAN LOOK AT IT. IT'S PROBABLY JUST KIDS, ANYWAY.
WHY DO YOU ALWAYS BLAME KIDS FOR STUFF LIKE THIS? I SAW WHO DID THIS. HE HAD GRAY HAIR, AS IN AN OLD PERSON!
CHECK YOUR E-MAIL. THE PHOTO IS THERE.
BZZZZ BZZZ
YOU SENT A PHOTO TO MY PHONE!? HOW'D YOU DO THAT?
HAHAHA HAHAHA
HEY, CLARENCE. YOU GOTTA SEE WHAT THIS KID DID TO MY PHONE!

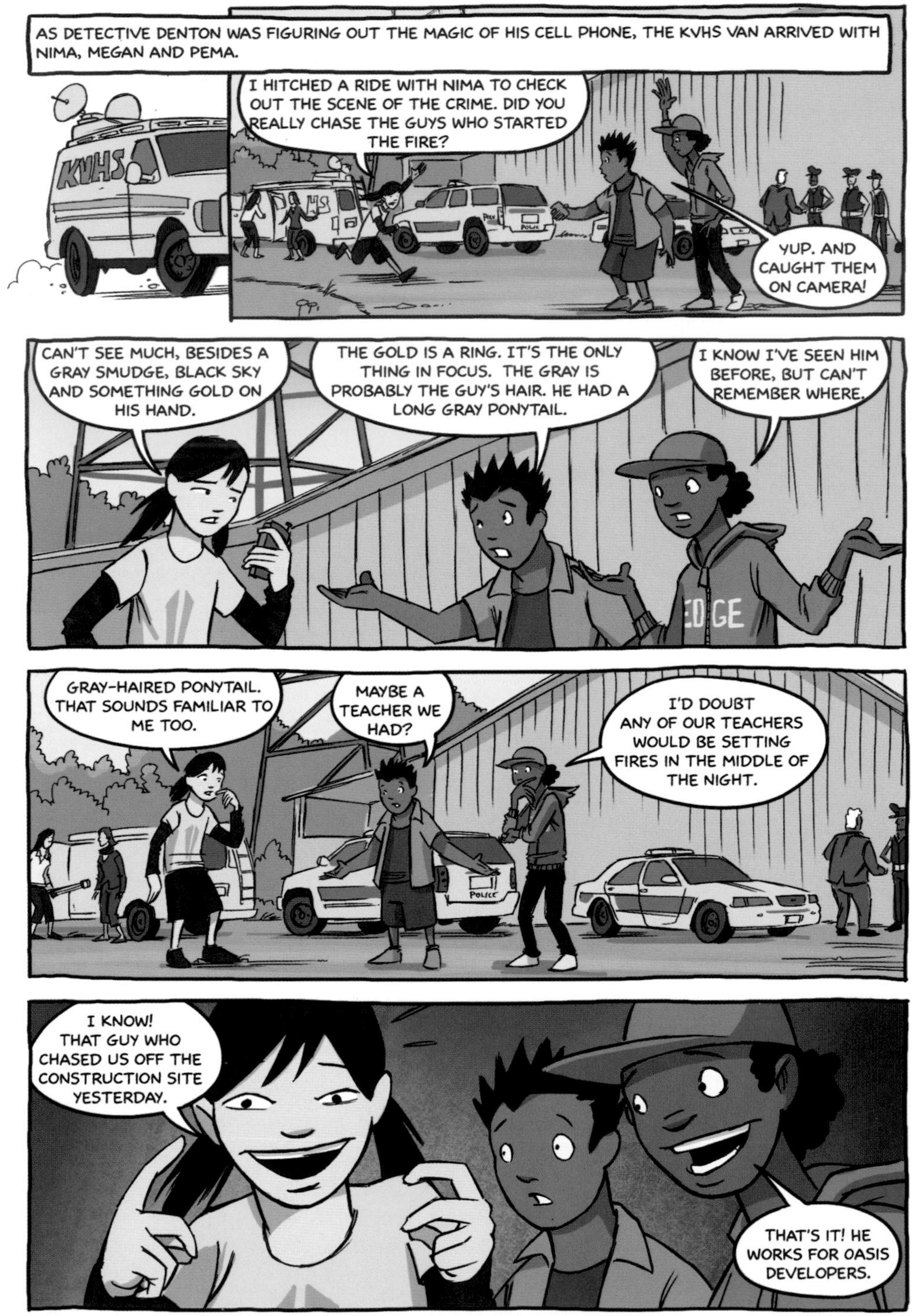
AS DETECTIVE DENTON WAS FIGURING OUT THE MAGIC OF HIS CELL PHONE, THE KVHS VAN ARRIVED WITH NIMA, MEGAN AND PEMA.
KVHS
I HITCHED A RIDE WITH NIMA TO CHECK OUT THE SCENE OF THE CRIME. DID YOU REALLY CHASE THE GUYS WHO STARTED THE FIRE?
YUP. AND CAUGHT THEM ON CAMERA!
CAN'T SEE MUCH, BESIDES A GRAY SMUDGE, BLACK SKY AND SOMETHING GOLD ON HIS HAND.
THE GOLD IS A RING. IT'S THE ONLY THING IN FOCUS. THE GRAY IS PROBABLY THE GUY'S HAIR. HE HAD A LONG GRAY PONYTAIL.
I KNOW I'VE SEEN HIM BEFORE, BUT CAN'T REMEMBER WHERE.
GRAY-HAIRED PONYTAIL. THAT SOUNDS FAMILIAR TO ME TOO.
MAYBE A TEACHER WE HAD?
I'D DOUBT ANY OF OUR TEACHERS WOULD BE SETTING FIRES IN THE MIDDLE OF THE NIGHT.
I KNOW! THAT GUY WHO CHASED US OFF THE CONSTRUCTION SITE YESTERDAY.
THAT'S IT! HE WORKS FOR OASIS DEVELOPERS.

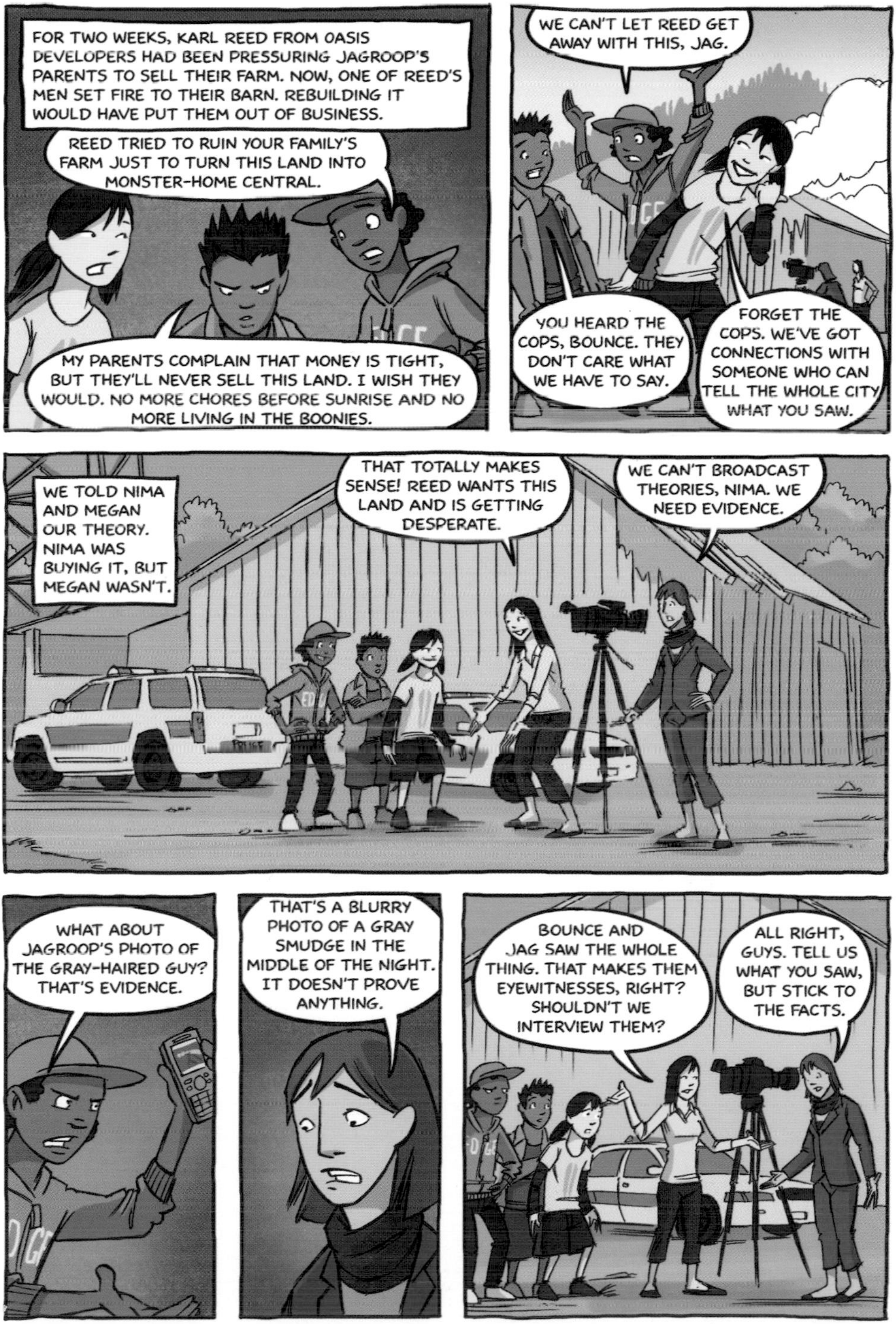
FOR TWO WEEKS, KARL REED FROM OASIS DEVELOPERS HAD BEEN PRESSURING JAGROOP'S PARENTS TO SELL THEIR FARM. NOW, ONE OF REED'S MEN SET FIRE TO THEIR BARN. REBUILDING IT WOULD HAVE PUT THEM OUT OF BUSINESS.
REED TRIED TO RUIN YOUR FAMILY'S FARM JUST TO TURN THIS LAND INTO MONSTER-HOME CENTRAL.
MY PARENTS COMPLAIN THAT MONEY IS TIGHT, BUT THEY'LL NEVER SELL THIS LAND. I WISH THEY WOULD. NO MORE CHORES BEFORE SUNRISE AND NO MORE LIVING IN THE BOONIES.
WE CAN'T LET REED GET AWAY WITH THIS, JAG.
YOU HEARD THE COPS, BOUNCE. THEY DON'T CARE WHAT WE HAVE TO SAY.
FORGET THE COPS. WE'VE GOT CONNECTIONS WITH SOMEONE WHO CAN TELL THE WHOLE CITY WHAT YOU SAW.
WE TOLD NIMA AND MEGAN OUR THEORY. NIMA WAS BUYING IT, BUT MEGAN WASN'T.
THAT TOTALLY MAKES SENSE! REED WANTS THIS LAND AND IS GETTING DESPERATE.
WE CAN'T BROADCAST THEORIES, NIMA. WE NEED EVIDENCE.
WHAT ABOUT JAGROOP'S PHOTO OF THE GRAY-HAIRED GUY? THAT'S EVIDENCE.
THAT'S A BLURRY PHOTO OF A GRAY SMUDGE IN THE MIDDLE OF THE NIGHT. IT DOESN'T PROVE ANYTHING.
BOUNCE AND JAG SAW THE WHOLE THING. THAT MAKES THEM EYEWITNESSES, RIGHT? SHOULDN'T WE INTERVIEW THEM?
ALL RIGHT, GUYS. TELL US WHAT YOU SAW, BUT STICK TO THE FACTS.

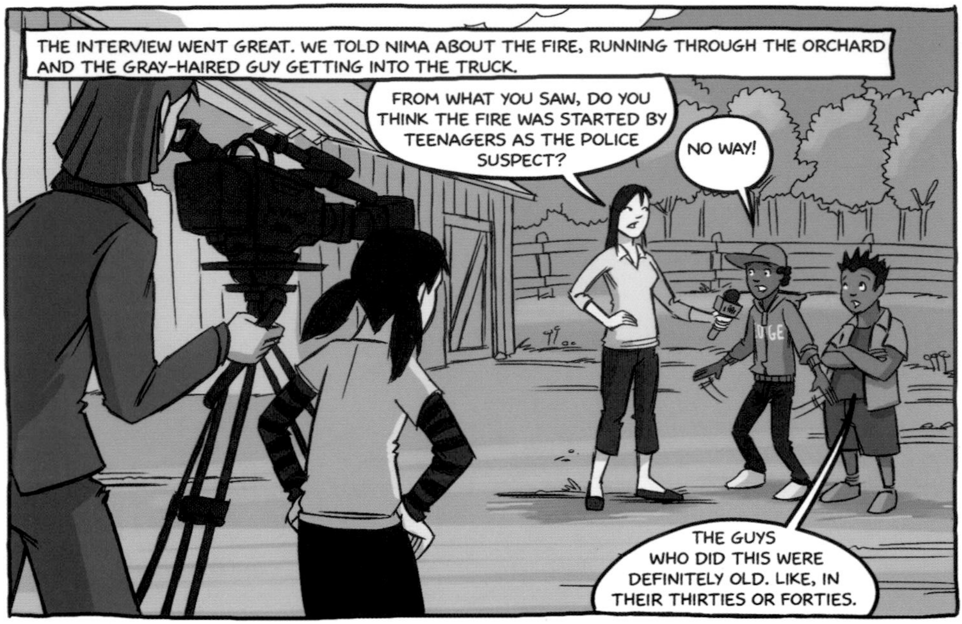
THE INTERVIEW WENT GREAT. WE TOLD NIMA ABOUT THE FIRE, RUNNING THROUGH THE ORCHARD AND THE GRAY-HAIRED GUY GETTING INTO THE TRUCK.
FROM WHAT YOU SAW, DO YOU THINK THE FIRE WAS STARTED BY TEENAGERS AS THE POLICE SUSPECT?
NO WAY!
THE GUYS WHO DID THIS WERE DEFINITELY OLD. LIKE, IN THEIR THIRTIES OR FORTIES.

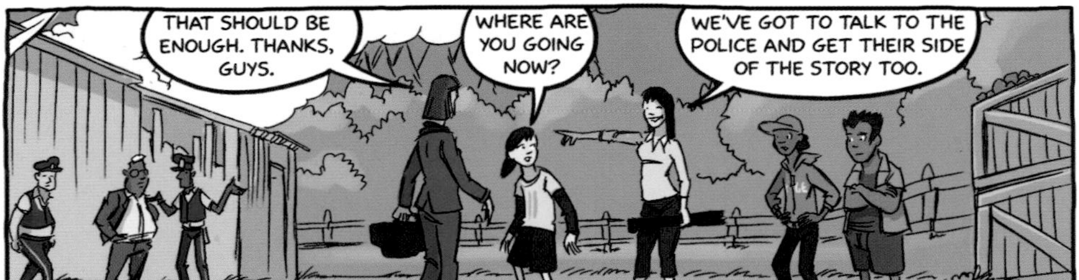
THAT SHOULD BE ENOUGH. THANKS, GUYS.
WHERE ARE YOU GOING NOW?
WE'VE GOT TO TALK TO THE POLICE AND GET THEIR SIDE OF THE STORY TOO.

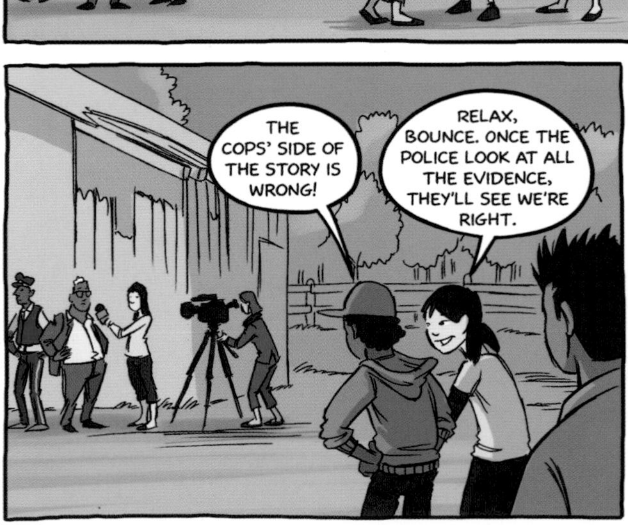
THE COPS' SIDE OF THE STORY IS WRONG!
RELAX, BOUNCE. ONCE THE POLICE LOOK AT ALL THE EVIDENCE, THEY'LL SEE WE'RE RIGHT.

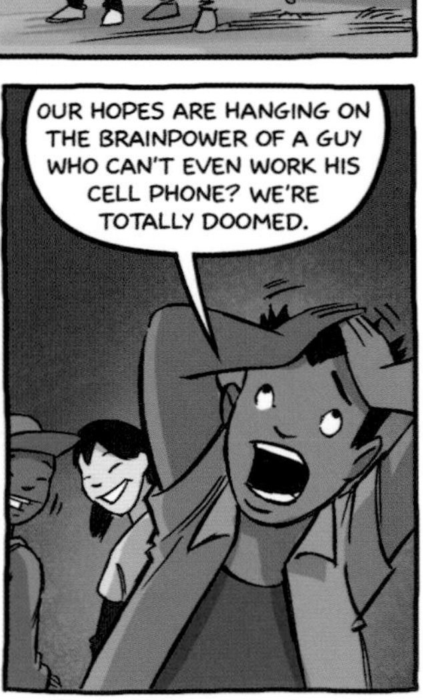
OUR HOPES ARE HANGING ON THE BRAINPOWER OF A GUY WHO CAN'T EVEN WORK HIS CELL PHONE? WE'RE TOTALLY DOOMED.

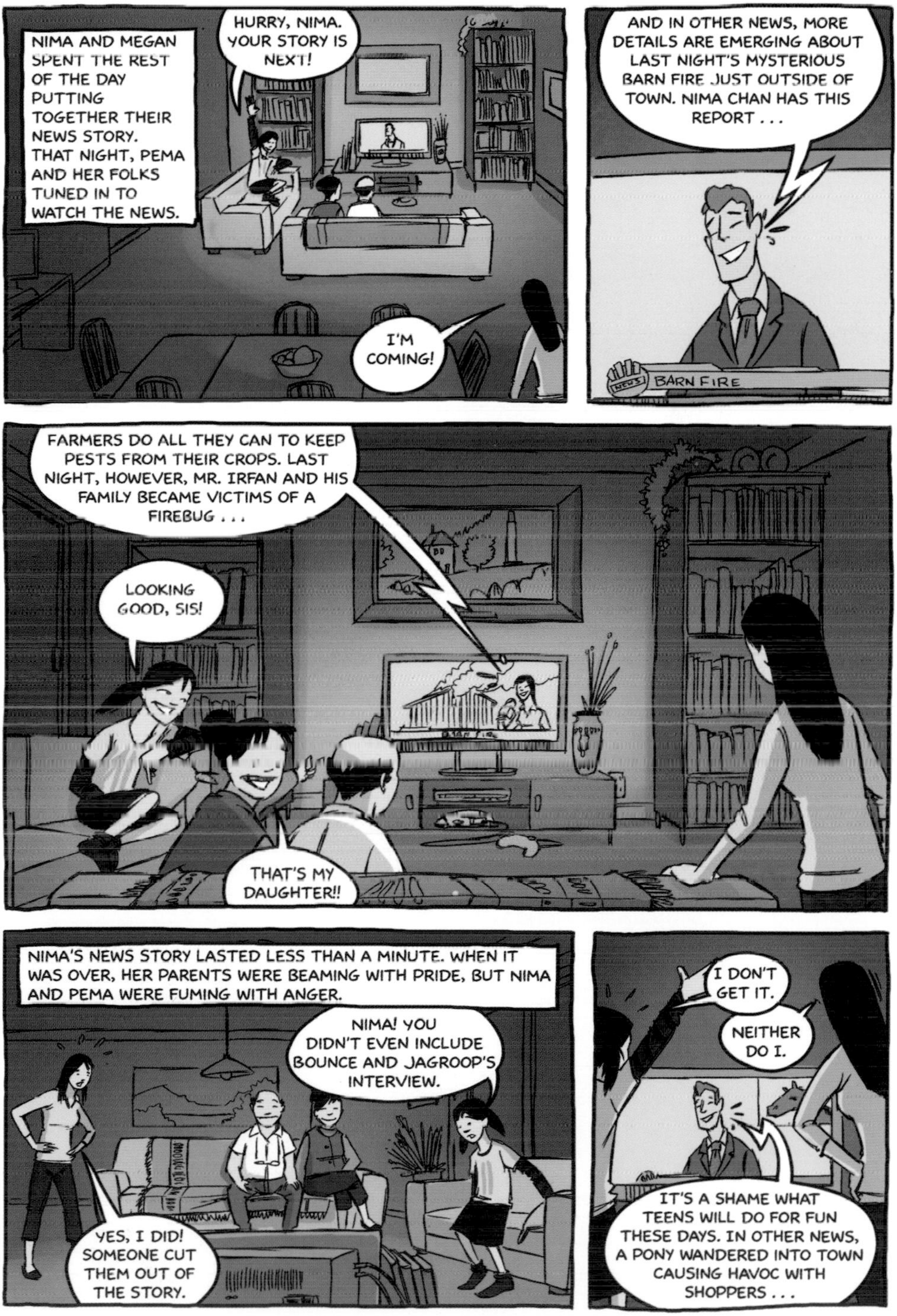
NIMA AND MEGAN SPENT THE REST OF THE DAY PUTTING TOGETHER THEIR NEWS STORY. THAT NIGHT, PEMA AND HER FOLKS TUNED IN TO WATCH THE NEWS.
HURRY, NIMA. YOUR STORY IS NEXT!
I'M COMING!
AND IN OTHER NEWS, MORE DETAILS ARE EMERGING ABOUT LAST NIGHT'S MYSTERIOUS BARN FIRE JUST OUTSIDE OF TOWN. NIMA CHAN HAS THIS REPORT . . .
NEWS
BARN FIRE
FARMERS DO ALL THEY CAN TO KEEP PESTS FROM THEIR CROPS. LAST NIGHT, HOWEVER, MR. IRFAN AND HIS FAMILY BECAME VICTIMS OF A FIREBUG . . .
LOOKING GOOD, SIS!
THAT'S MY DAUGHTER!!
NIMA'S NEWS STORY LASTED LESS THAN A MINUTE. WHEN IT WAS OVER, HER PARENTS WERE BEAMING WITH PRIDE, BUT NIMA AND PEMA WERE FUMING WITH ANGER.
NIMA! YOU DIDN'T EVEN INCLUDE BOUNCE AND JAGROOP'S INTERVIEW.
YES, I DID! SOMEONE CUT THEM OUT OF THE STORY.
I DON'T GET IT.
NEITHER DO I.
IT'S A SHAME WHAT TEENS WILL DO FOR FUN THESE DAYS. IN OTHER NEWS, A PONY WANDERED INTO TOWN CAUSING HAVOC WITH SHOPPERS . . .

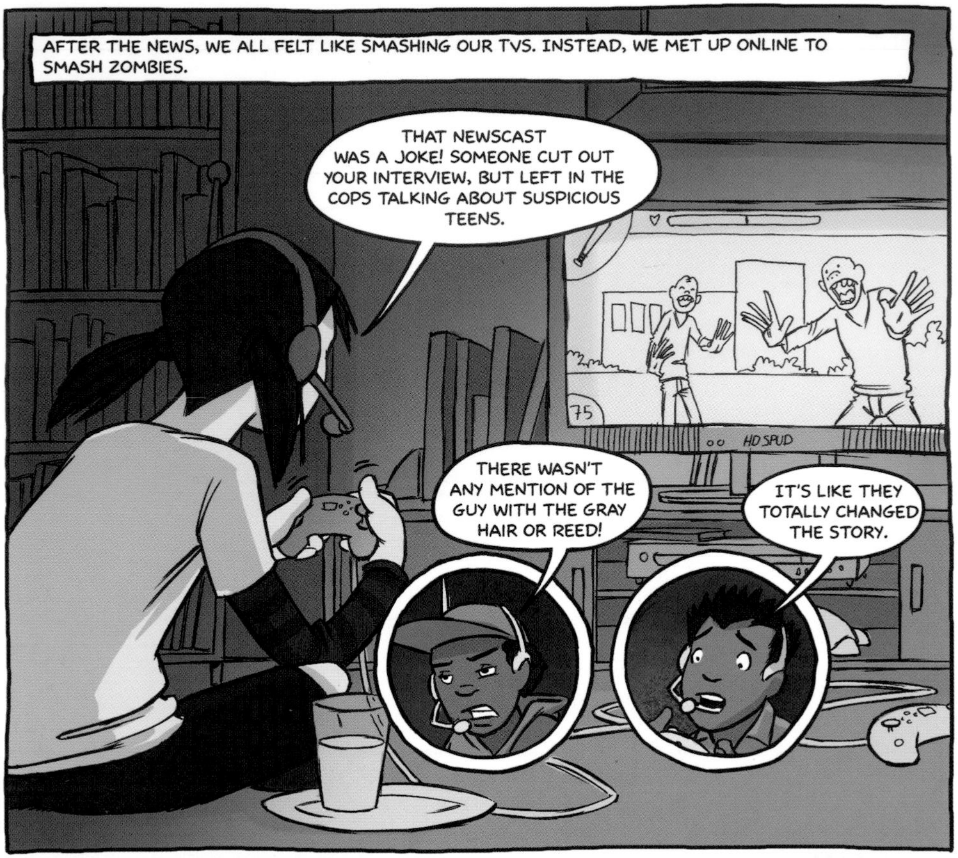
AFTER THE NEWS, WE ALL FELT LIKE SMASHING OUR TVS. INSTEAD, WE MET UP ONLINE TO SMASH ZOMBIES.
THAT NEWSCAST WAS A JOKE! SOMEONE CUT OUT YOUR INTERVIEW, BUT LEFT IN THE COPS TALKING ABOUT SUSPICIOUS TEENS.
75
HD SPUD
THERE WASN'T ANY MENTION OF THE GUY WITH THE GRAY HAIR OR REED!
IT'S LIKE THEY TOTALLY CHANGED THE STORY.

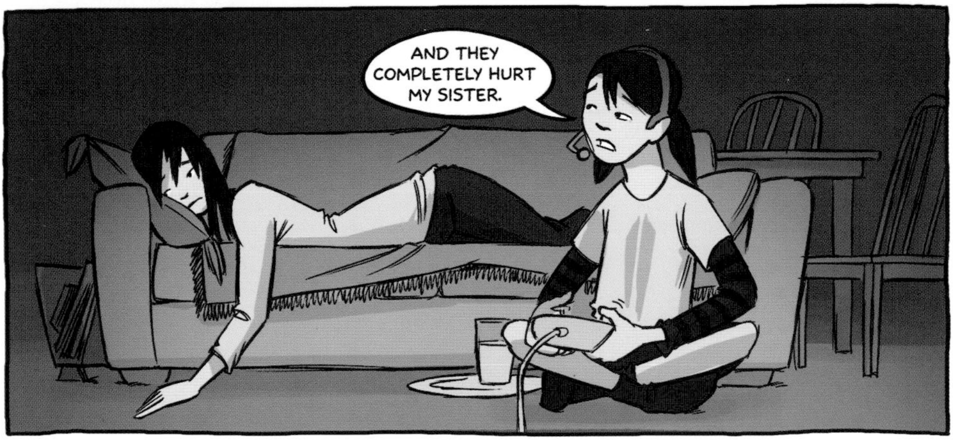
AND THEY COMPLETELY HURT MY SISTER.

CHAPTER 3
HOOK, CREEP AND FILTER

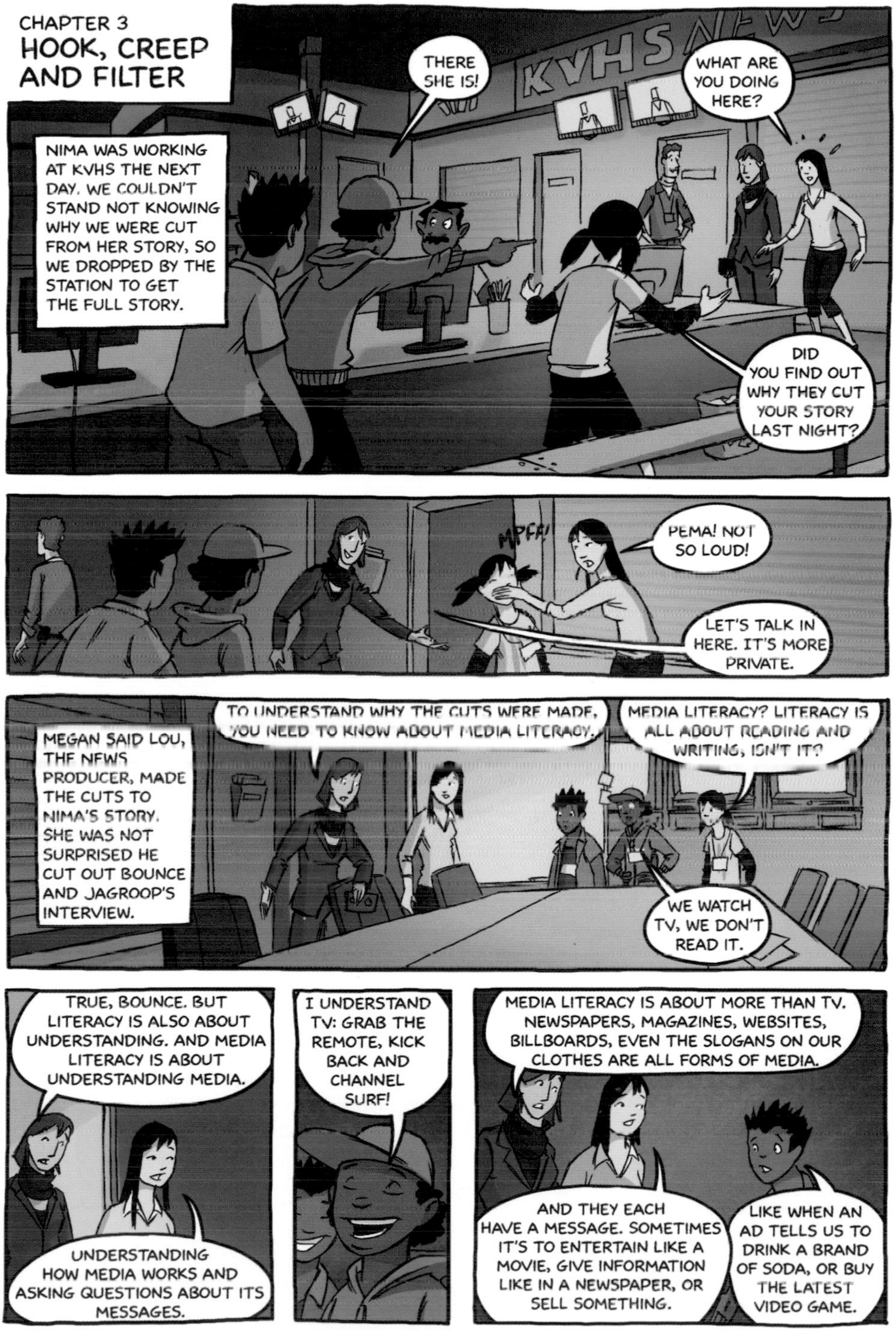
NIMA WAS WORKING AT KVHS THE NEXT DAY. WE COULDN'T STAND NOT KNOWING WHY WE WERE CUT FROM HER STORY, SO WE DROPPED BY THE STATION TO GET THE FULL STORY.
THERE SHE IS!
KVHS NEWS
WHAT ARE YOU DOING HERE?
DID YOU FIND OUT WHY THEY CUT YOUR STORY LAST NIGHT?
MPFF!
PEMA! NOT SO LOUD!
LET'S TALK IN HERE. IT'S MORE PRIVATE.
MEGAN SAID LOU, THE NEWS PRODUCER, MADE THE CUTS TO NIMA'S STORY. SHE WAS NOT SURPRISED HE CUT OUT BOUNCE AND JAGROOP'S INTERVIEW.
TO UNDERSTAND WHY THE CUTS WERE MADE, YOU NEED TO KNOW ABOUT MEDIA LITERACY.
MEDIA LITERACY? LITERACY IS ALL ABOUT READING AND WRITING, ISN'T IT?
WE WATCH TV, WE DON'T READ IT.
TRUE, BOUNCE. BUT LITERACY IS ALSO ABOUT UNDERSTANDING. AND MEDIA LITERACY IS ABOUT UNDERSTANDING MEDIA.
UNDERSTANDING HOW MEDIA WORKS AND ASKING QUESTIONS ABOUT ITS MESSAGES.
I UNDERSTAND TV: GRAB THE REMOTE, KICK BACK AND CHANNEL SURF!
MEDIA LITERACY IS ABOUT MORE THAN TV. NEWSPAPERS, MAGAZINES, WEBSITES, BILLBOARDS, EVEN THE SLOGANS ON OUR CLOTHES ARE ALL FORMS OF MEDIA.
AND THEY EACH HAVE A MESSAGE. SOMETIMES IT'S TO ENTERTAIN LIKE A MOVIE, GIVE INFORMATION LIKE IN A NEWSPAPER, OR SELL SOMETHING.
LIKE WHEN AN AD TELLS US TO DRINK A BRAND OF SODA, OR BUY THE LATEST VIDEO GAME.

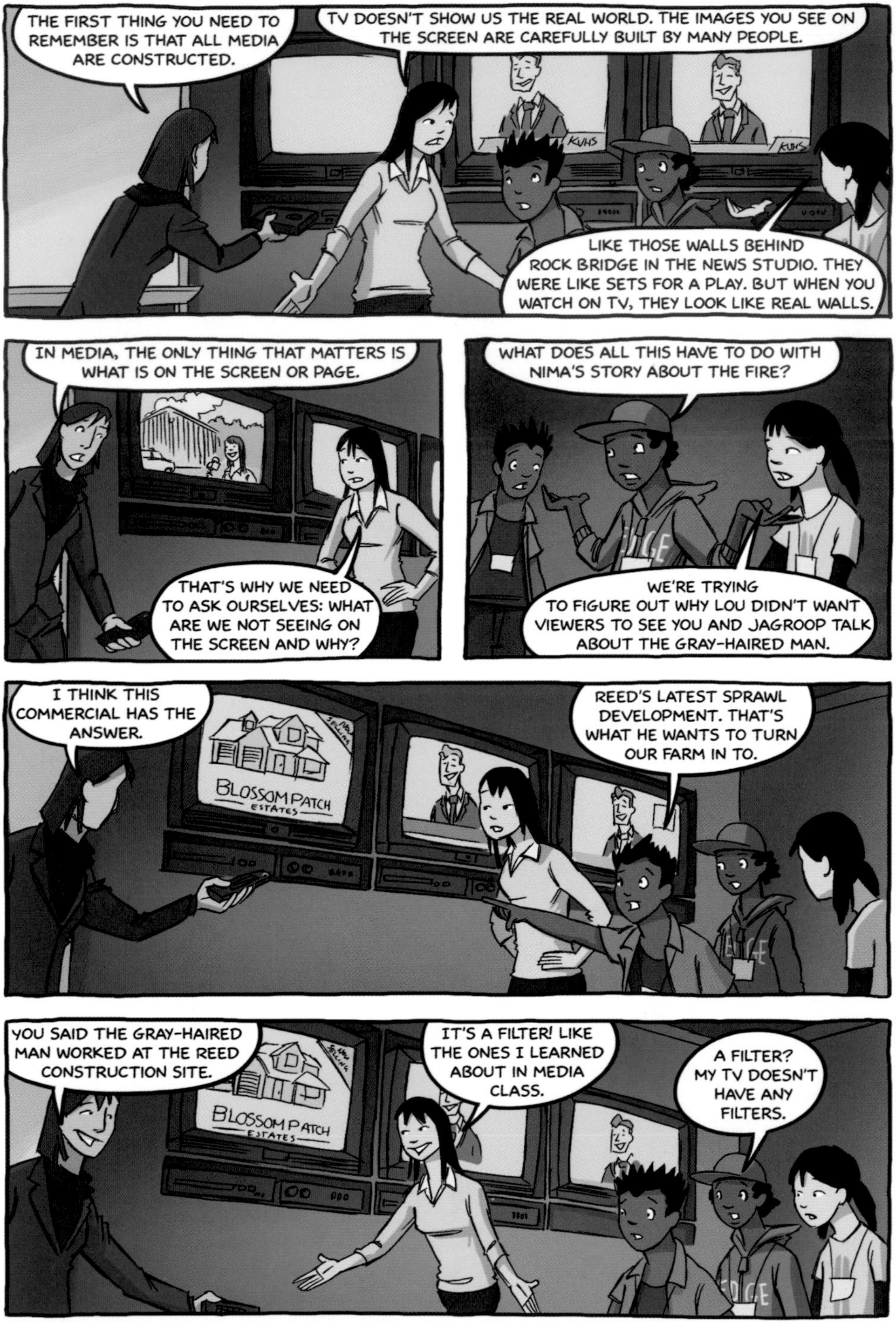
THE FIRST THING YOU NEED TO REMEMBER IS THAT ALL MEDIA ARE CONSTRUCTED.
TV DOESN'T SHOW US THE REAL WORLD. THE IMAGES YOU SEE ON THE SCREEN ARE CAREFULLY BUILT BY MANY PEOPLE.
KUHS
KUHS
LIKE THOSE WALLS BEHIND ROCK BRIDGE IN THE NEWS STUDIO. THEY WERE LIKE SETS FOR A PLAY. BUT WHEN YOU WATCH ON TV, THEY LOOK LIKE REAL WALLS.
IN MEDIA, THE ONLY THING THAT MATTERS IS WHAT IS ON THE SCREEN OR PAGE.
THAT'S WHY WE NEED TO ASK OURSELVES: WHAT ARE WE NOT SEEING ON THE SCREEN AND WHY?
WHAT DOES ALL THIS HAVE TO DO WITH NIMA'S STORY ABOUT THE FIRE?
WE'RE TRYING TO FIGURE OUT WHY LOU DIDN'T WANT VIEWERS TO SEE YOU AND JAGROOP TALK ABOUT THE GRAY-HAIRED MAN.
I THINK THIS COMMERCIAL HAS THE ANSWER.
BLOSSOM PATCH ESTATES
REED'S LATEST SPRAWL DEVELOPMENT. THAT'S WHAT HE WANTS TO TURN OUR FARM IN TO.
YOU SAID THE GRAY-HAIRED MAN WORKED AT THE REED CONSTRUCTION SITE.
BLOSSOM PATCH ESTATES
IT'S A FILTER! LIKE THE ONES I LEARNED ABOUT IN MEDIA CLASS.
A FILTER? MY TV DOESN'T HAVE ANY FILTERS.

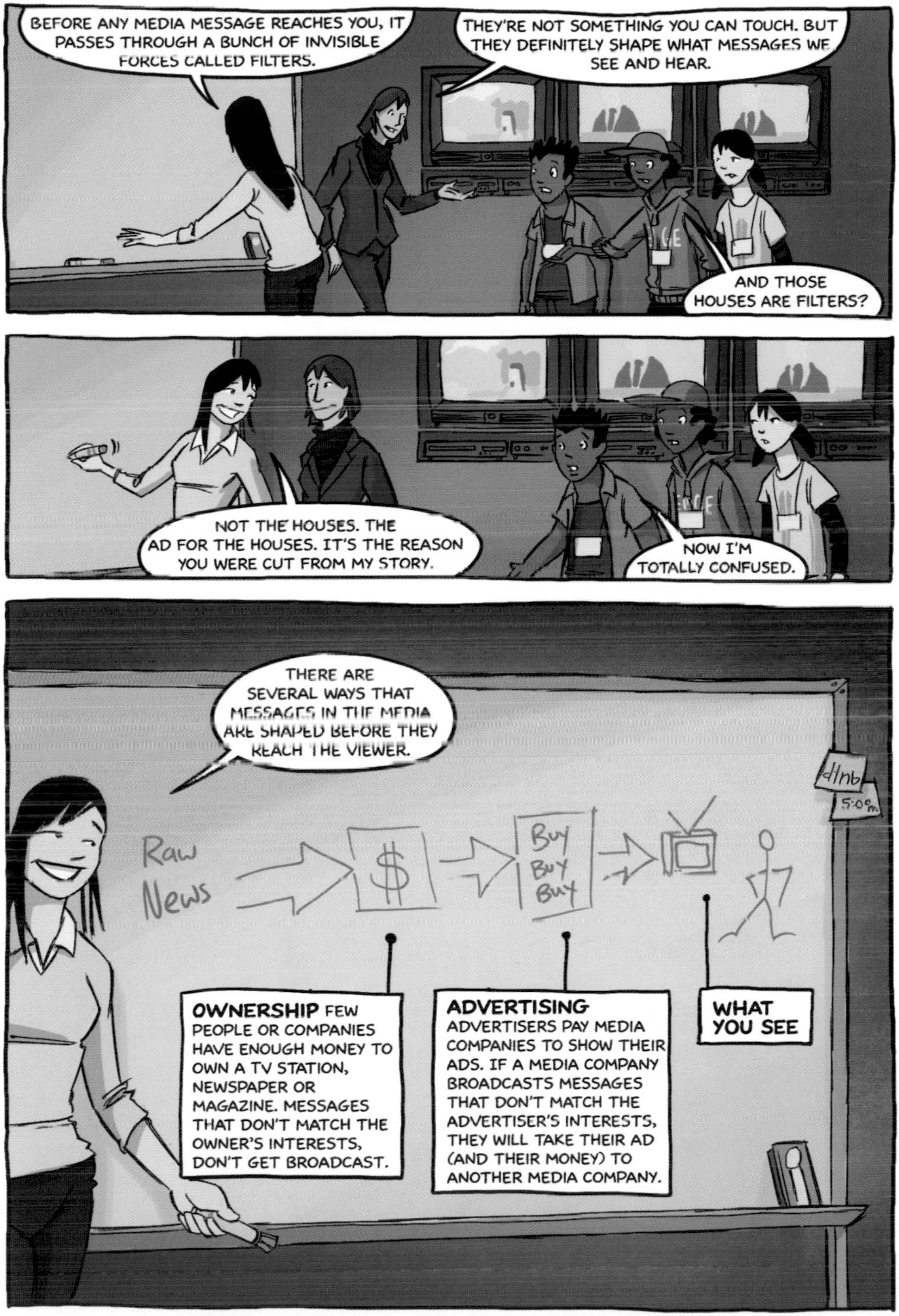
BEFORE ANY MEDIA MESSAGE REACHES YOU, IT PASSES THROUGH A BUNCH OF INVISIBLE FORCES CALLED FILTERS.
THEY'RE NOT SOMETHING YOU CAN TOUCH. BUT THEY DEFINITELY SHAPE WHAT MESSAGES WE SEE AND HEAR.
AND THOSE HOUSES ARE FILTERS?
NOT THE HOUSES. THE AD FOR THE HOUSES. IT'S THE REASON YOU WERE CUT FROM MY STORY.
NOW I'M TOTALLY CONFUSED.
THERE ARE SEVERAL WAYS THAT MESSAGES IN THE MEDIA ARE SHAPED BEFORE THEY REACH THE VIEWER.
Raw News
$
Buy Buy Buy
OWNERSHIP FEW PEOPLE OR COMPANIES HAVE ENOUGH MONEY TO OWN A TV STATION, NEWSPAPER OR MAGAZINE. MESSAGES THAT DON'T MATCH THE OWNER'S INTERESTS, DON'T GET BROADCAST.
ADVERTISING ADVERTISERS PAY MEDIA COMPANIES TO SHOW THEIR ADS. IF A MEDIA COMPANY BROADCASTS MESSAGES THAT DON'T MATCH THE ADVERTISER'S INTERESTS, THEY WILL TAKE THEIR AD (AND THEIR MONEY) TO ANOTHER MEDIA COMPANY.
WHAT YOU SEE

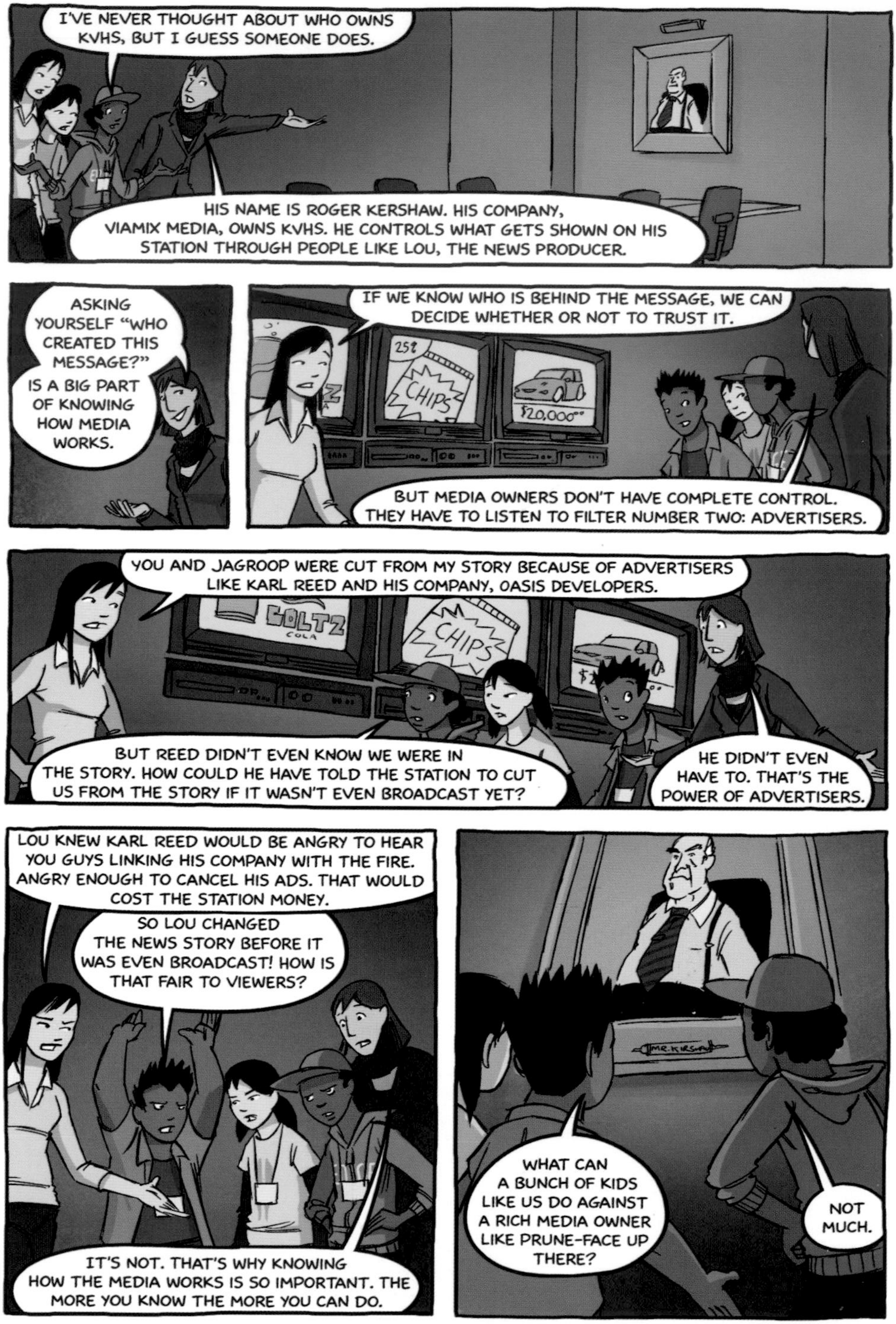
I'VE NEVER THOUGHT ABOUT WHO OWNS KVHS, BUT I GUESS SOMEONE DOES.
HIS NAME IS ROGER KERSHAW. HIS COMPANY, VIAMIX MEDIA, OWNS KVHS. HE CONTROLS WHAT GETS SHOWN ON HIS STATION THROUGH PEOPLE LIKE LOU, THE NEWS PRODUCER.
ASKING YOURSELF "WHO CREATED THIS MESSAGE?" IS A BIG PART OF KNOWING HOW MEDIA WORKS.
IF WE KNOW WHO IS BEHIND THE MESSAGE, WE CAN DECIDE WHETHER OR NOT TO TRUST IT.
25¢
CHIPS
$20,000
BUT MEDIA OWNERS DON'T HAVE COMPLETE CONTROL. THEY HAVE TO LISTEN TO FILTER NUMBER TWO: ADVERTISERS.
YOU AND JAGROOP WERE CUT FROM MY STORY BECAUSE OF ADVERTISERS LIKE KARL REED AND HIS COMPANY, OASIS DEVELOPERS.
COLTZ COLA
CHIPS
BUT REED DIDN'T EVEN KNOW WE WERE IN THE STORY. HOW COULD HE HAVE TOLD THE STATION TO CUT US FROM THE STORY IF IT WASN'T EVEN BROADCAST YET?
HE DIDN'T EVEN HAVE TO. THAT'S THE POWER OF ADVERTISERS.
LOU KNEW KARL REED WOULD BE ANGRY TO HEAR YOU GUYS LINKING HIS COMPANY WITH THE FIRE. ANGRY ENOUGH TO CANCEL HIS ADS. THAT WOULD COST THE STATION MONEY.
SO LOU CHANGED THE NEWS STORY BEFORE IT WAS EVEN BROADCAST! HOW IS THAT FAIR TO VIEWERS?
IT'S NOT. THAT'S WHY KNOWING HOW THE MEDIA WORKS IS SO IMPORTANT. THE MORE YOU KNOW THE MORE YOU CAN DO.
WHAT CAN A BUNCH OF KIDS LIKE US DO AGAINST A RICH MEDIA OWNER LIKE PRUNE-FACE UP THERE?
NOT MUCH.

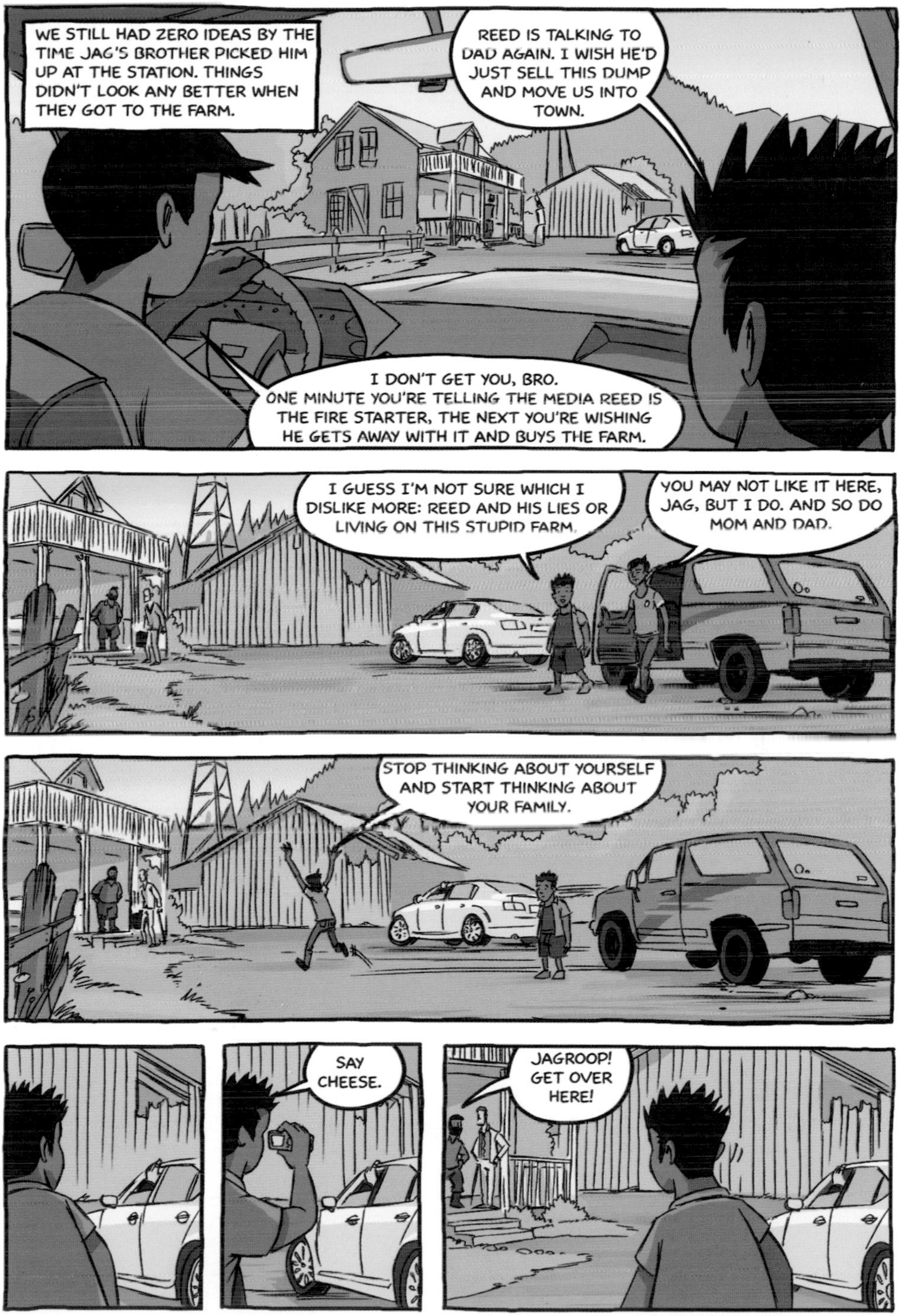
WE STILL HAD ZERO IDEAS BY THE TIME JAG'S BROTHER PICKED HIM UP AT THE STATION. THINGS DIDN'T LOOK ANY BETTER WHEN THEY GOT TO THE FARM.
REED IS TALKING TO DAD AGAIN. I WISH HE'D JUST SELL THIS DUMP AND MOVE US INTO TOWN.
I DON'T GET YOU, BRO. ONE MINUTE YOU'RE TELLING THE MEDIA REED IS THE FIRE STARTER, THE NEXT YOU'RE WISHING HE GETS AWAY WITH IT AND BUYS THE FARM.
I GUESS I'M NOT SURE WHICH I DISLIKE MORE: REED AND HIS LIES OR LIVING ON THIS STUPID FARM.
YOU MAY NOT LIKE IT HERE, JAG, BUT I DO. AND SO DO MOM AND DAD.
STOP THINKING ABOUT YOURSELF AND START THINKING ABOUT YOUR FAMILY.
SAY CHEESE.
JAGROOP! GET OVER HERE!

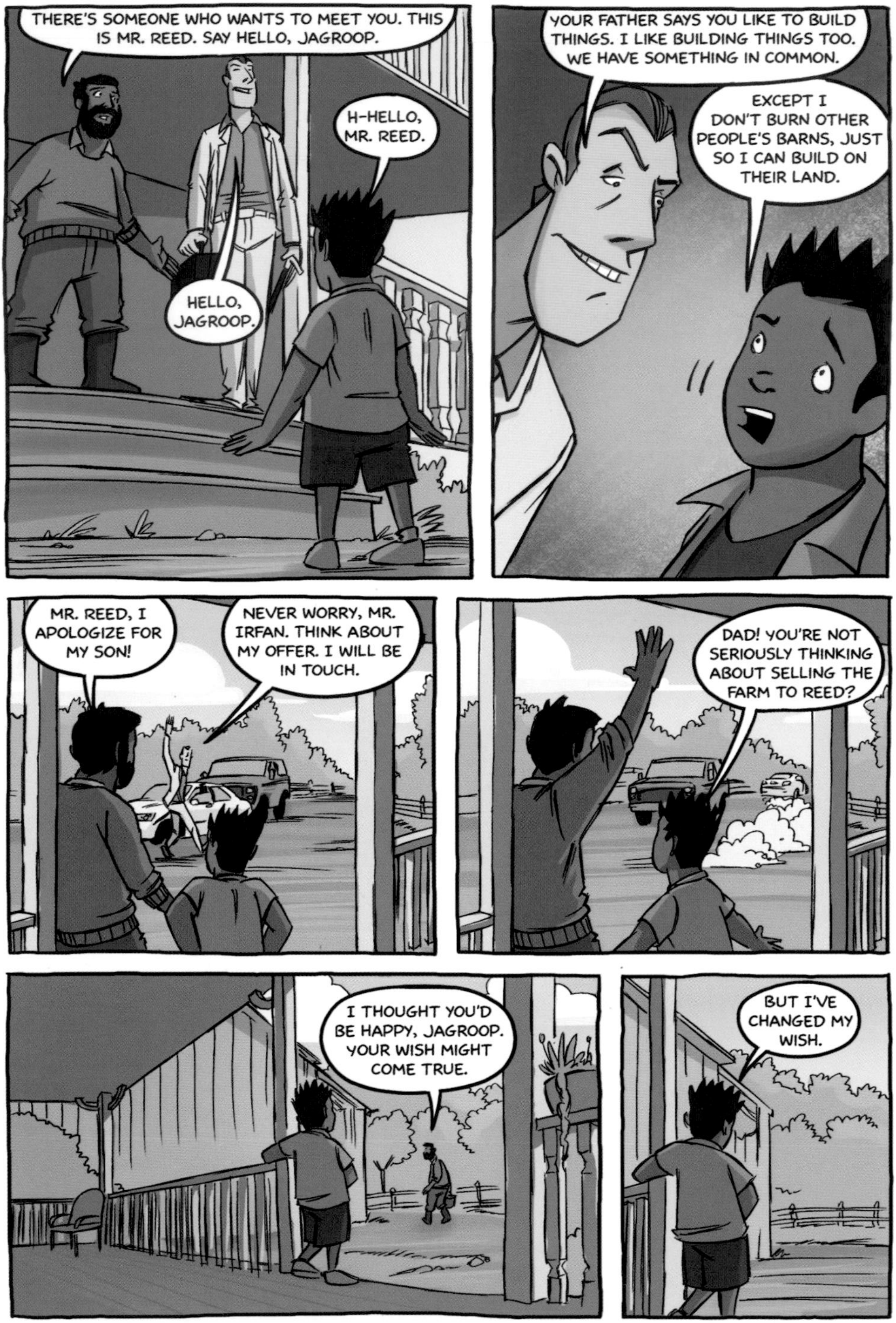
THERE'S SOMEONE WHO WANTS TO MEET YOU. THIS IS MR. REED. SAY HELLO, JAGROOP.
H-HELLO, MR. REED.
HELLO, JAGROOP.
YOUR FATHER SAYS YOU LIKE TO BUILD THINGS. I LIKE BUILDING THINGS TOO. WE HAVE SOMETHING IN COMMON.
EXCEPT I DON'T BURN OTHER PEOPLE'S BARNS, JUST SO I CAN BUILD ON THEIR LAND.
MR. REED, I APOLOGIZE FOR MY SON!
NEVER WORRY, MR. IRFAN. THINK ABOUT MY OFFER. I WILL BE IN TOUCH.
DAD! YOU'RE NOT SERIOUSLY THINKING ABOUT SELLING THE FARM TO REED?
I THOUGHT YOU'D BE HAPPY, JAGROOP. YOUR WISH MIGHT COME TRUE.
BUT I'VE CHANGED MY WISH.

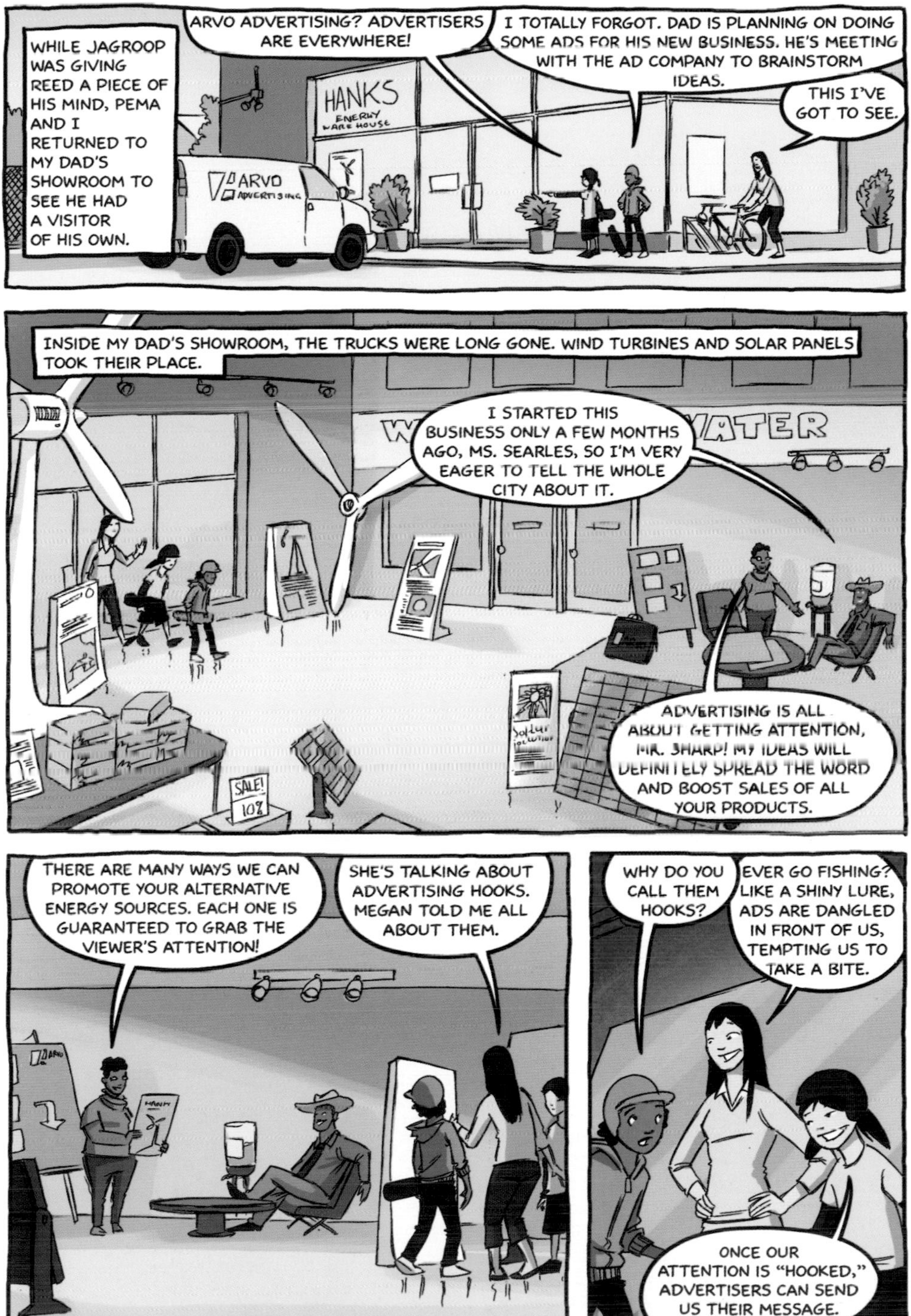
WHILE JAGROOP WAS GIVING REED A PIECE OF HIS MIND, PEMA AND I RETURNED TO MY DAD'S SHOWROOM TO SEE HE HAD A VISITOR OF HIS OWN.
ARVO ADVERTISING? ADVERTISERS ARE EVERYWHERE!
I TOTALLY FORGOT. DAD IS PLANNING ON DOING SOME ADS FOR HIS NEW BUSINESS. HE'S MEETING WITH THE AD COMPANY TO BRAINSTORM IDEAS.
THIS I'VE GOT TO SEE.
HANKS
ENERGY WAREHOUSE
ARVO ADVERTISING
INSIDE MY DAD'S SHOWROOM, THE TRUCKS WERE LONG GONE. WIND TURBINES AND SOLAR PANELS TOOK THEIR PLACE.
I STARTED THIS BUSINESS ONLY A FEW MONTHS AGO, MS. SEARLES, SO I'M VERY EAGER TO TELL THE WHOLE CITY ABOUT IT.
ADVERTISING IS ALL ABOUT GETTING ATTENTION, MR. SHARP! MY IDEAS WILL DEFINITELY SPREAD THE WORD AND BOOST SALES OF ALL YOUR PRODUCTS.
SALE!
10%
THERE ARE MANY WAYS WE CAN PROMOTE YOUR ALTERNATIVE ENERGY SOURCES. EACH ONE IS GUARANTEED TO GRAB THE VIEWER'S ATTENTION!
SHE'S TALKING ABOUT ADVERTISING HOOKS. MEGAN TOLD ME ALL ABOUT THEM.
WHY DO YOU CALL THEM HOOKS?
EVER GO FISHING? LIKE A SHINY LURE, ADS ARE DANGLED IN FRONT OF US, TEMPTING US TO TAKE A BITE.
ONCE OUR ATTENTION IS "HOOKED," ADVERTISERS CAN SEND US THEIR MESSAGE.

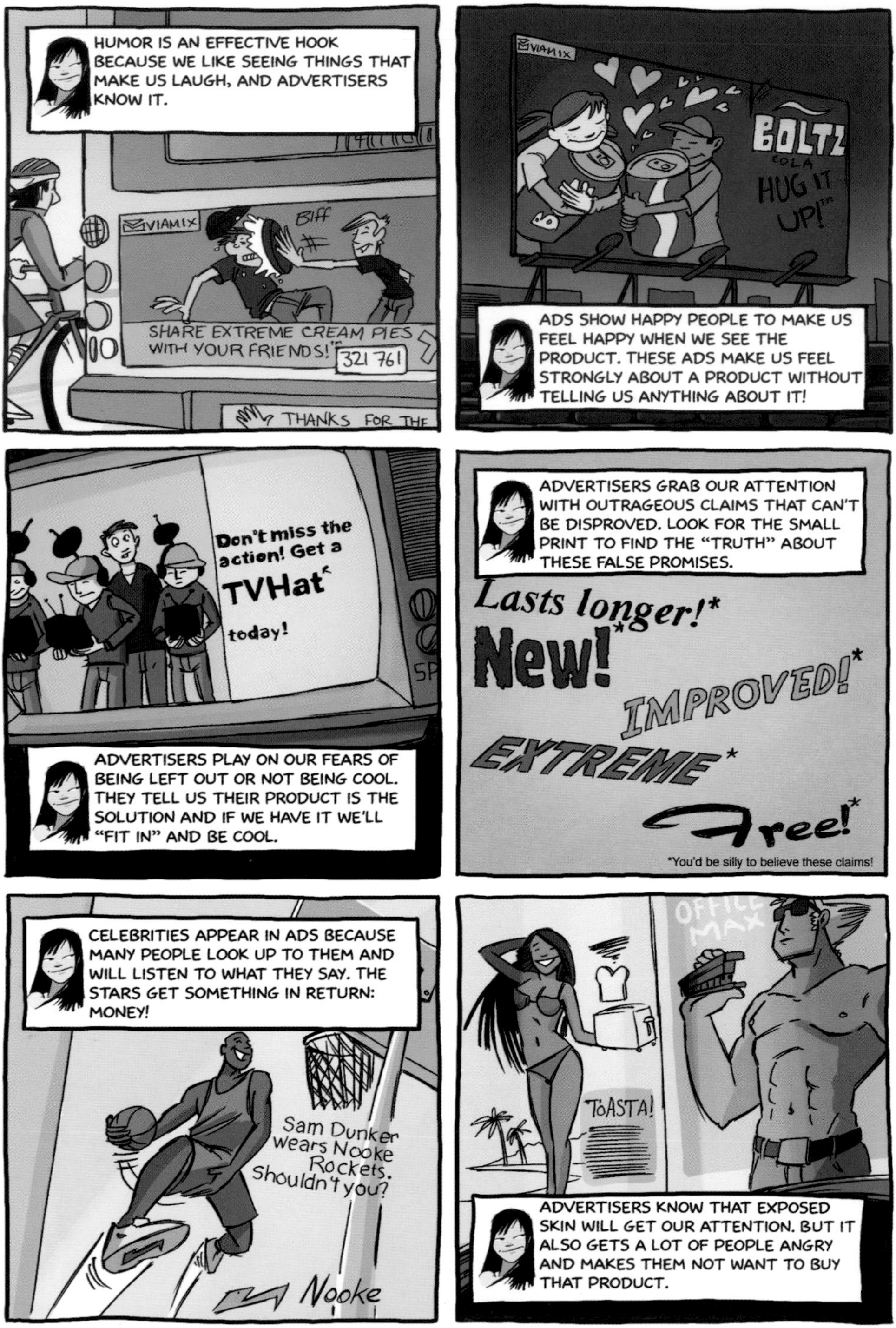
HUMOR IS AN EFFECTIVE HOOK BECAUSE WE LIKE SEEING THINGS THAT MAKE US LAUGH, AND ADVERTISERS KNOW IT.
VIAMIX
Biff
SHARE EXTREME CREAM PIES WITH YOUR FRIENDS!™
321 761
THANKS FOR THE
VIAMIX
BOLTZ
COLA
HUG IT UP!™
ADS SHOW HAPPY PEOPLE TO MAKE US FEEL HAPPY WHEN WE SEE THE PRODUCT. THESE ADS MAKE US FEEL STRONGLY ABOUT A PRODUCT WITHOUT TELLING US ANYTHING ABOUT IT!
Don't miss the action! Get a TVHat today!
ADVERTISERS PLAY ON OUR FEARS OF BEING LEFT OUT OR NOT BEING COOL. THEY TELL US THEIR PRODUCT IS THE SOLUTION AND IF WE HAVE IT WE'LL "FIT IN" AND BE COOL.
ADVERTISERS GRAB OUR ATTENTION WITH OUTRAGEOUS CLAIMS THAT CAN'T BE DISPROVED. LOOK FOR THE SMALL PRINT TO FIND THE "TRUTH" ABOUT THESE FALSE PROMISES.
Lasts longer!*
New!*
IMPROVED!*
EXTREME*
Free!*
*You'd be silly to believe these claims!
CELEBRITIES APPEAR IN ADS BECAUSE MANY PEOPLE LOOK UP TO THEM AND WILL LISTEN TO WHAT THEY SAY. THE STARS GET SOMETHING IN RETURN: MONEY!
Sam Dunker wears Nooke Rockets. Shouldn't you?
Nooke
OFFICE MAX
TOASTA!
ADVERTISERS KNOW THAT EXPOSED SKIN WILL GET OUR ATTENTION. BUT IT ALSO GETS A LOT OF PEOPLE ANGRY AND MAKES THEM NOT WANT TO BUY THAT PRODUCT.

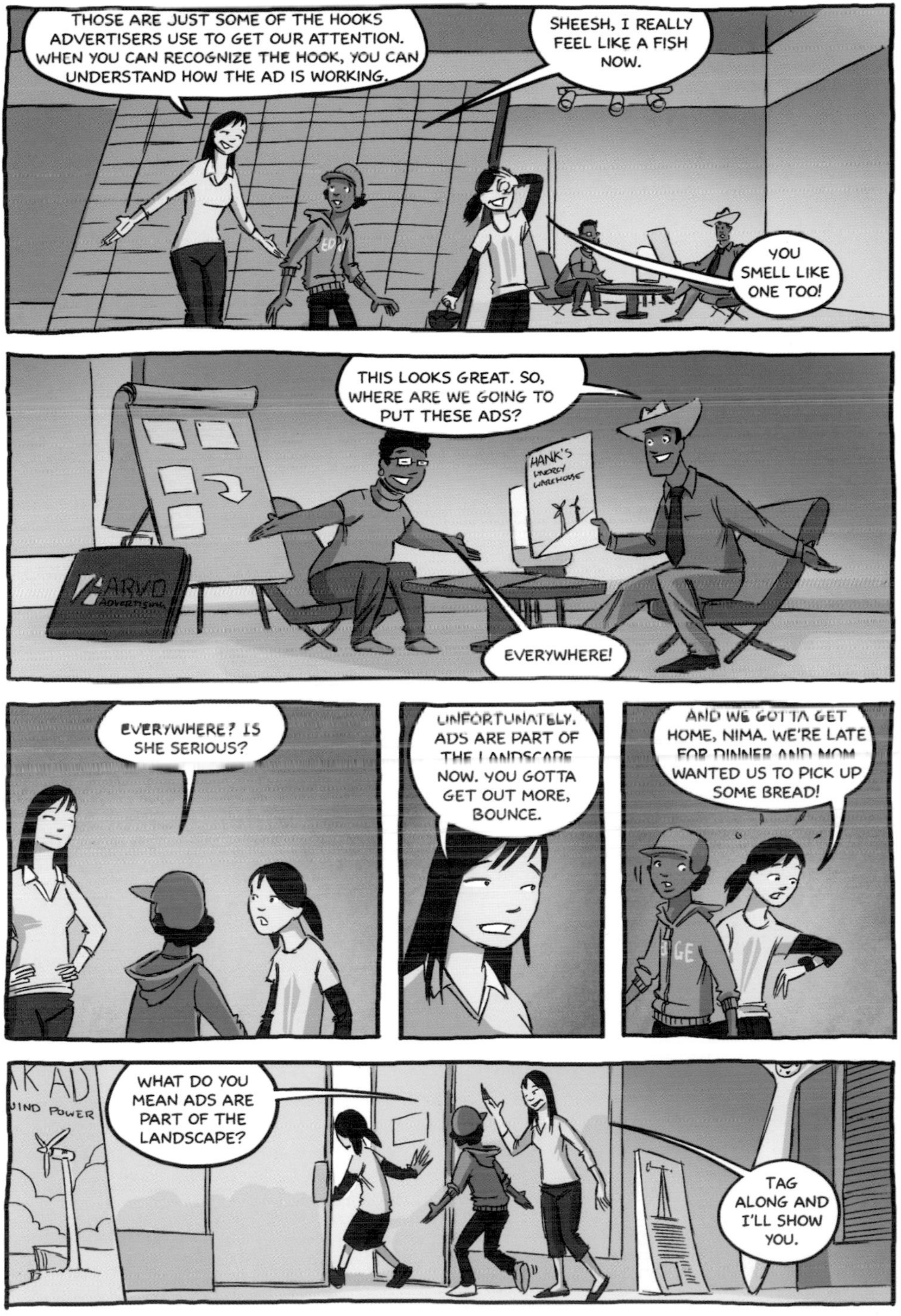
THOSE ARE JUST SOME OF THE HOOKS ADVERTISERS USE TO GET OUR ATTENTION. WHEN YOU CAN RECOGNIZE THE HOOK, YOU CAN UNDERSTAND HOW THE AD IS WORKING.
SHEESH, I REALLY FEEL LIKE A FISH NOW.
YOU SMELL LIKE ONE TOO!
THIS LOOKS GREAT. SO, WHERE ARE WE GOING TO PUT THESE ADS?
HANK'S
EVERYWHERE!
EVERYWHERE? IS SHE SERIOUS?
UNFORTUNATELY, ADS ARE PART OF THE LANDSCAPE NOW. YOU GOTTA GET OUT MORE, BOUNCE.
AND WE GOTTA GET HOME, NIMA. WE'RE LATE FOR DINNER AND MOM WANTED US TO PICK UP SOME BREAD!
WHAT DO YOU MEAN ADS ARE PART OF THE LANDSCAPE?
WIND POWER
TAG ALONG AND I'LL SHOW YOU.

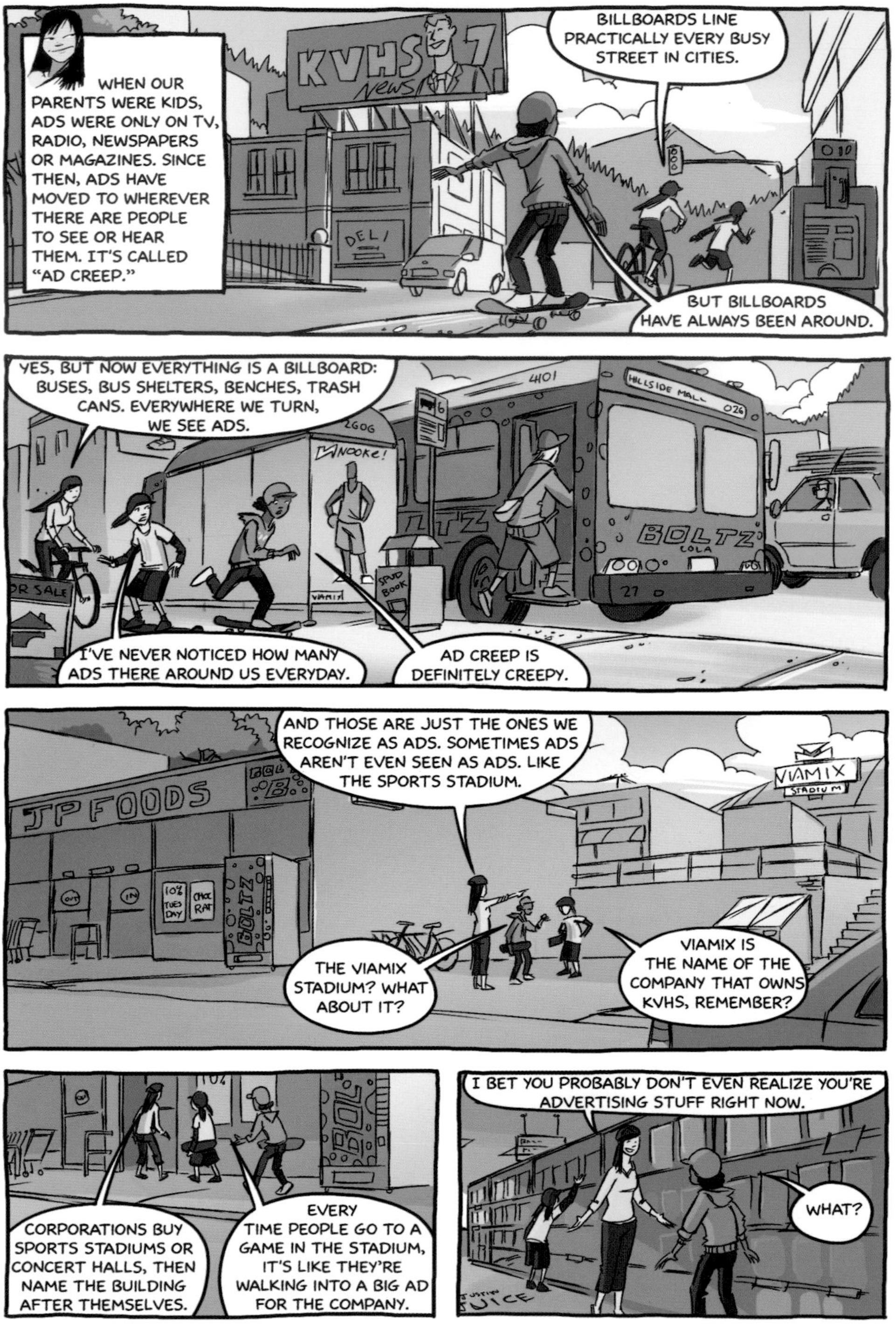
WHEN OUR PARENTS WERE KIDS, ADS WERE ONLY ON TV, RADIO, NEWSPAPERS OR MAGAZINES. SINCE THEN, ADS HAVE MOVED TO WHEREVER THERE ARE PEOPLE TO SEE OR HEAR THEM. IT'S CALLED "AD CREEP."
KVHS 7 News
DELI
BILLBOARDS LINE PRACTICALLY EVERY BUSY STREET IN CITIES.
BUT BILLBOARDS HAVE ALWAYS BEEN AROUND.
YES, BUT NOW EVERYTHING IS A BILLBOARD: BUSES, BUS SHELTERS, BENCHES, TRASH CANS. EVERYWHERE WE TURN, WE SEE ADS.
HILLSIDE MALL
BOLTZ COLA
I'VE NEVER NOTICED HOW MANY ADS THERE AROUND US EVERYDAY.
AD CREEP IS DEFINITELY CREEPY.
JP FOODS
AND THOSE ARE JUST THE ONES WE RECOGNIZE AS ADS. SOMETIMES ADS AREN'T EVEN SEEN AS ADS. LIKE THE SPORTS STADIUM.
VIAMIX STADIUM
THE VIAMIX STADIUM? WHAT ABOUT IT?
VIAMIX IS THE NAME OF THE COMPANY THAT OWNS KVHS, REMEMBER?
CORPORATIONS BUY SPORTS STADIUMS OR CONCERT HALLS, THEN NAME THE BUILDING AFTER THEMSELVES.
EVERY TIME PEOPLE GO TO A GAME IN THE STADIUM, IT'S LIKE THEY'RE WALKING INTO A BIG AD FOR THE COMPANY.
I BET YOU PROBABLY DON'T EVEN REALIZE YOU'RE ADVERTISING STUFF RIGHT NOW.
WHAT?
JUSTIN JUICE

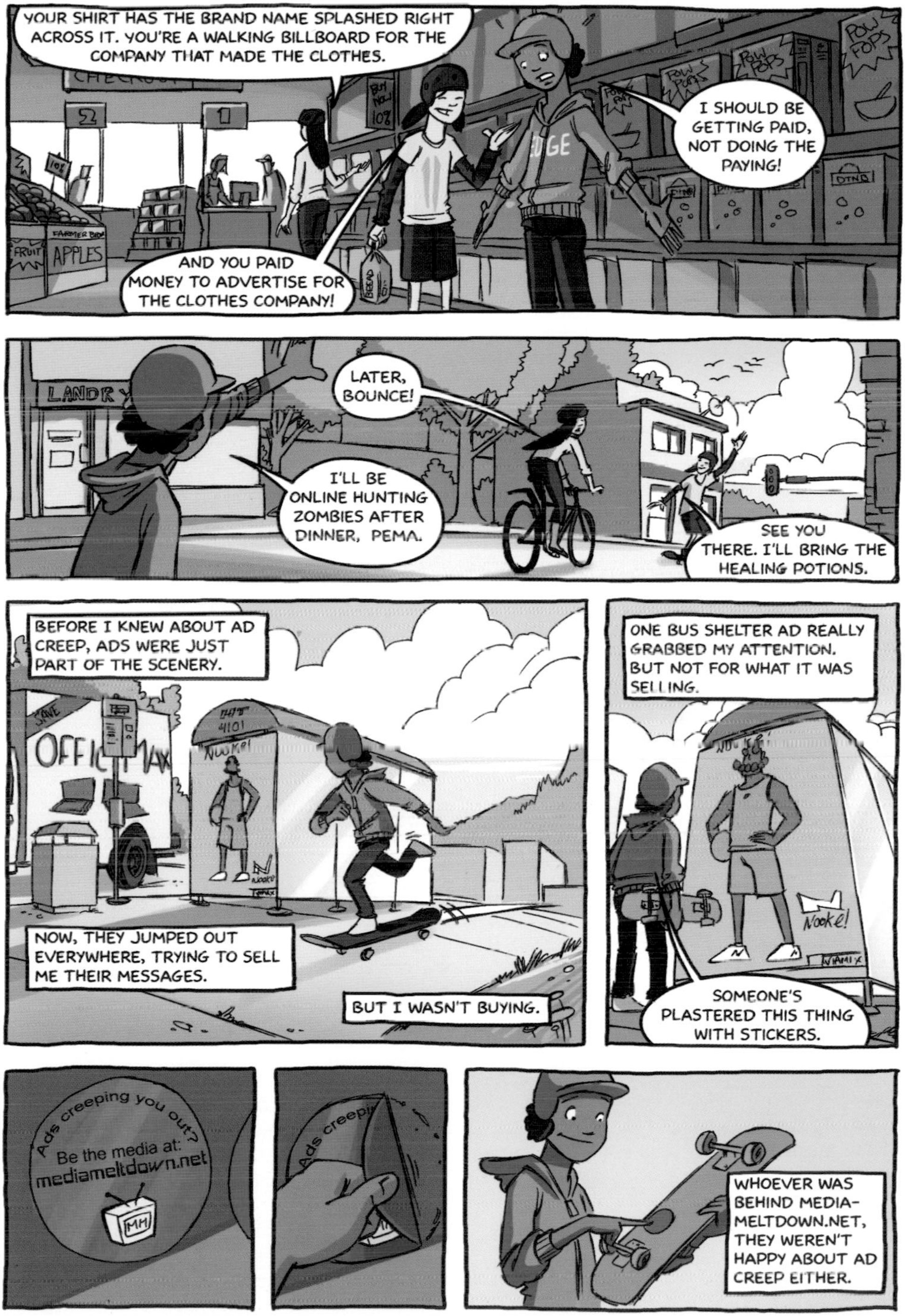
YOUR SHIRT HAS THE BRAND NAME SPLASHED RIGHT ACROSS IT. YOU'RE A WALKING BILLBOARD FOR THE COMPANY THAT MADE THE CLOTHES.
AND YOU PAID MONEY TO ADVERTISE FOR THE CLOTHES COMPANY!
I SHOULD BE GETTING PAID, NOT DOING THE PAYING!
LATER, BOUNCE!
I'LL BE ONLINE HUNTING ZOMBIES AFTER DINNER, PEMA.
SEE YOU THERE. I'LL BRING THE HEALING POTIONS.
BEFORE I KNEW ABOUT AD CREEP, ADS WERE JUST PART OF THE SCENERY.
NOW, THEY JUMPED OUT EVERYWHERE, TRYING TO SELL ME THEIR MESSAGES.
BUT I WASN'T BUYING.
ONE BUS SHELTER AD REALLY GRABBED MY ATTENTION. BUT NOT FOR WHAT IT WAS SELLING.
SOMEONE'S PLASTERED THIS THING WITH STICKERS.
Ads creeping you out?
Be the media at:
mediameltdown.net
MM
WHOEVER WAS BEHIND MEDIA-MELTDOWN.NET, THEY WEREN'T HAPPY ABOUT AD CREEP EITHER.

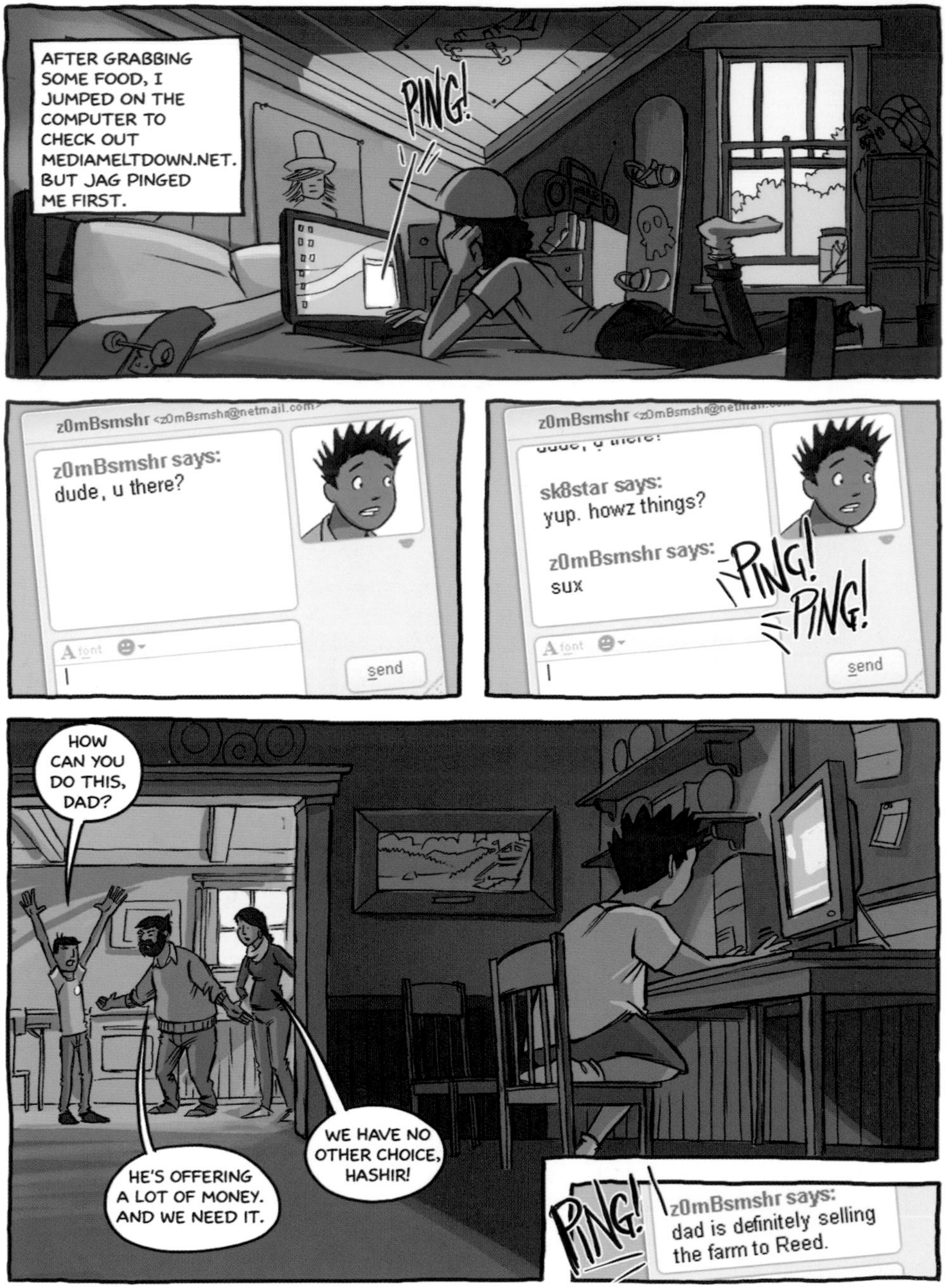
AFTER GRABBING SOME FOOD, I JUMPED ON THE COMPUTER TO CHECK OUT MEDIAMELTDOWN.NET. BUT JAG PINGED ME FIRST.
PING!
z0mBsmshr <z0mBsmshr@netmail.com>
z0mBsmshr says:
dude, u there?
font
send
z0mBsmshr
sk8star says:
yup. howz things?
z0mBsmshr says:
sux
PING!
PING!
send
HOW CAN YOU DO THIS, DAD?
HE'S OFFERING A LOT OF MONEY. AND WE NEED IT.
WE HAVE NO OTHER CHOICE, HASHIR!
PING!
z0mBsmshr says:
dad is definitely selling the farm to Reed.

CHAPTER 4
BEING MEDIA

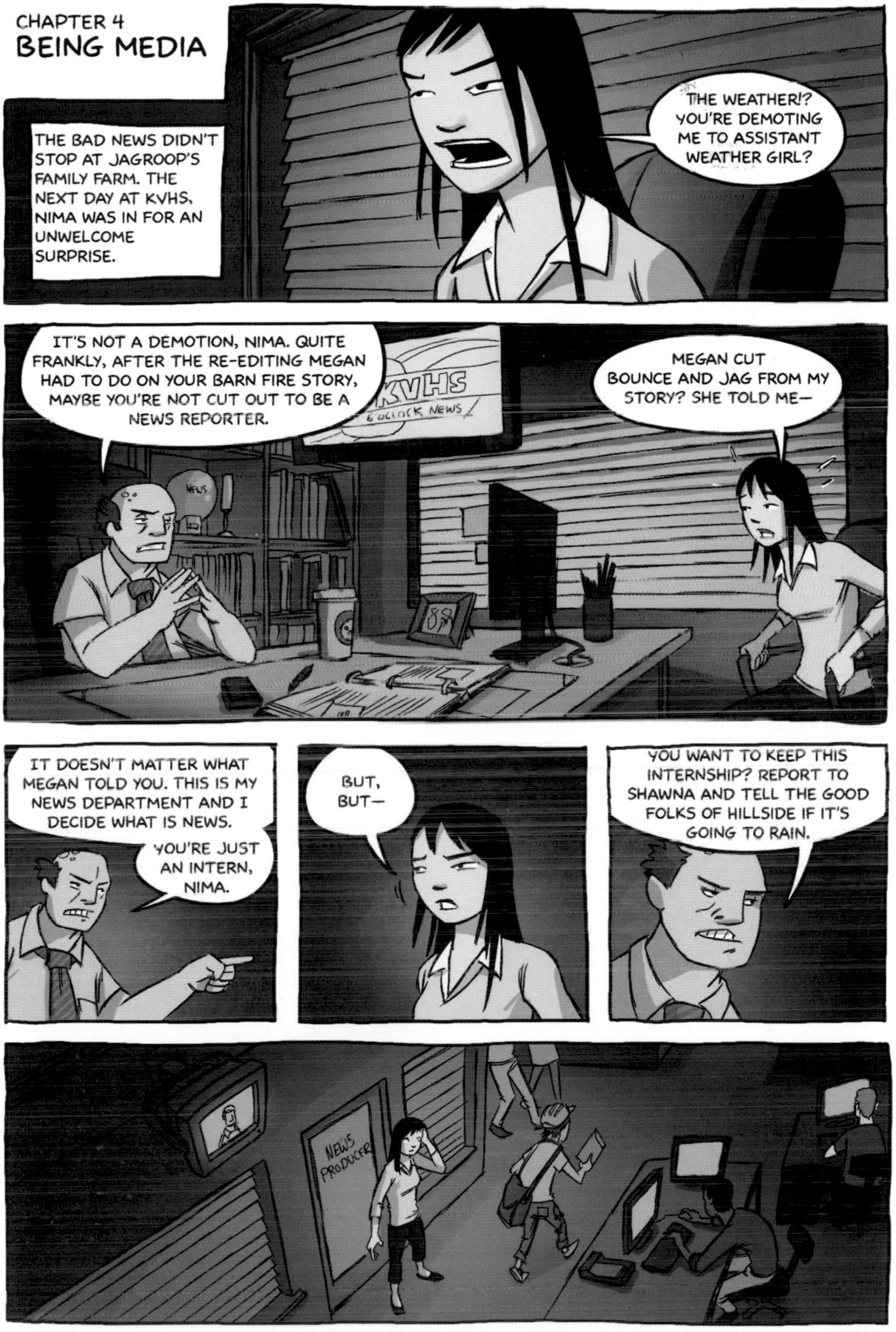
THE BAD NEWS DIDN'T STOP AT JAGROOP'S FAMILY FARM. THE NEXT DAY AT KVHS, NIMA WAS IN FOR AN UNWELCOME SURPRISE.
THE WEATHER!? YOU'RE DEMOTING ME TO ASSISTANT WEATHER GIRL?
IT'S NOT A DEMOTION, NIMA. QUITE FRANKLY, AFTER THE RE-EDITING MEGAN HAD TO DO ON YOUR BARN FIRE STORY, MAYBE YOU'RE NOT CUT OUT TO BE A NEWS REPORTER.
KVHS
NEWS
MEGAN CUT BOUNCE AND JAG FROM MY STORY? SHE TOLD ME—
IT DOESN'T MATTER WHAT MEGAN TOLD YOU. THIS IS MY NEWS DEPARTMENT AND I DECIDE WHAT IS NEWS.
YOU'RE JUST AN INTERN, NIMA.
BUT, BUT—
YOU WANT TO KEEP THIS INTERNSHIP? REPORT TO SHAWNA AND TELL THE GOOD FOLKS OF HILLSIDE IF IT'S GOING TO RAIN.
NEWS PRODUCER

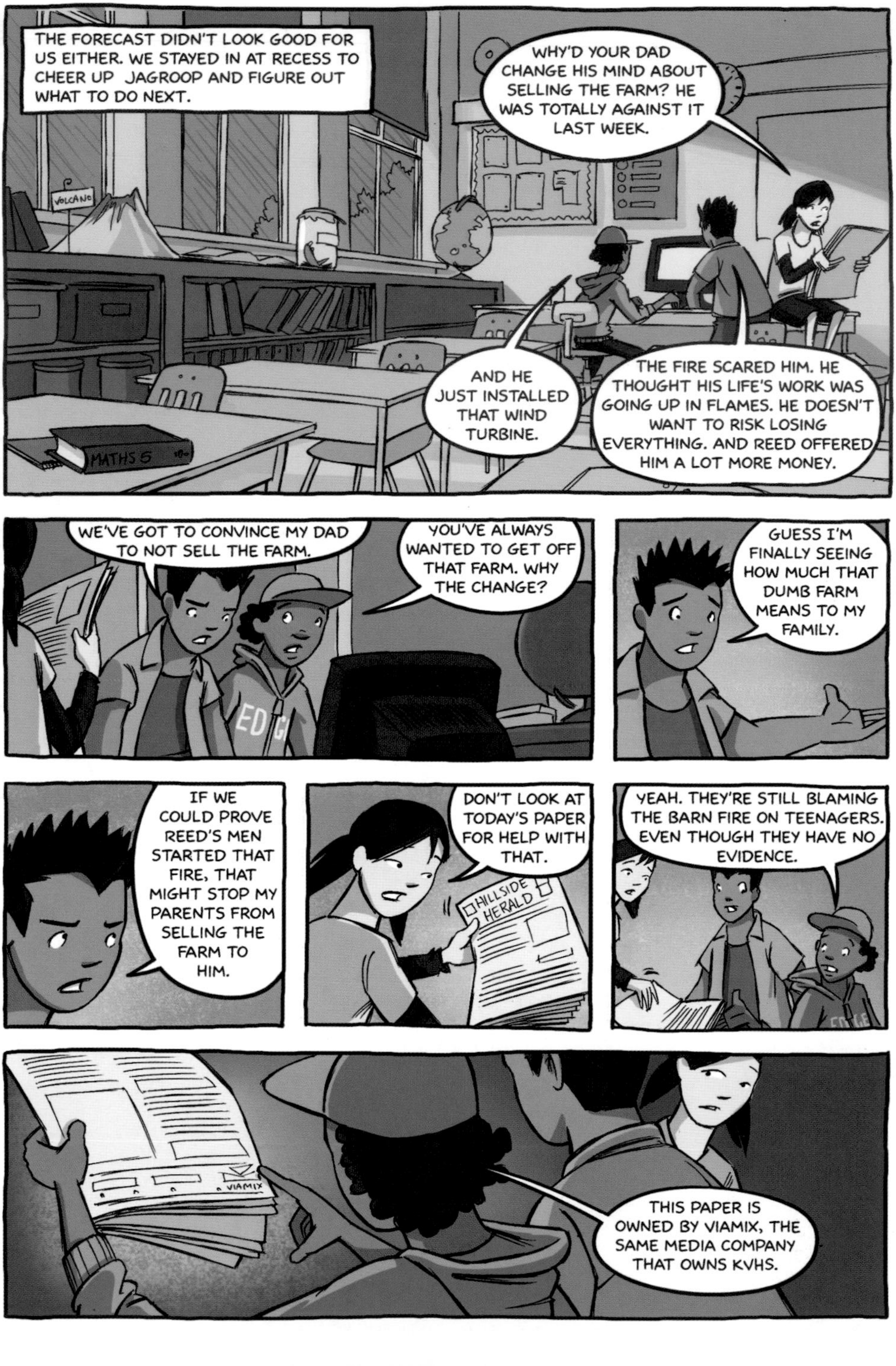

THE FORECAST DIDN'T LOOK GOOD FOR US EITHER. WE STAYED IN AT RECESS TO CHEER UP JAGROOP AND FIGURE OUT WHAT TO DO NEXT.
WHY'D YOUR DAD CHANGE HIS MIND ABOUT SELLING THE FARM? HE WAS TOTALLY AGAINST IT LAST WEEK.
VOLCANO
MATHS 5
AND HE JUST INSTALLED THAT WIND TURBINE.
THE FIRE SCARED HIM. HE THOUGHT HIS LIFE'S WORK WAS GOING UP IN FLAMES. HE DOESN'T WANT TO RISK LOSING EVERYTHING. AND REED OFFERED HIM A LOT MORE MONEY.
WE'VE GOT TO CONVINCE MY DAD TO NOT SELL THE FARM.
YOU'VE ALWAYS WANTED TO GET OFF THAT FARM. WHY THE CHANGE?
GUESS I'M FINALLY SEEING HOW MUCH THAT DUMB FARM MEANS TO MY FAMILY.
IF WE COULD PROVE REED'S MEN STARTED THAT FIRE, THAT MIGHT STOP MY PARENTS FROM SELLING THE FARM TO HIM.
DON'T LOOK AT TODAY'S PAPER FOR HELP WITH THAT.
HILLSIDE HERALD
YEAH. THEY'RE STILL BLAMING THE BARN FIRE ON TEENAGERS. EVEN THOUGH THEY HAVE NO EVIDENCE.
VIAMIX
THIS PAPER IS OWNED BY VIAMIX, THE SAME MEDIA COMPANY THAT OWNS KVHS.

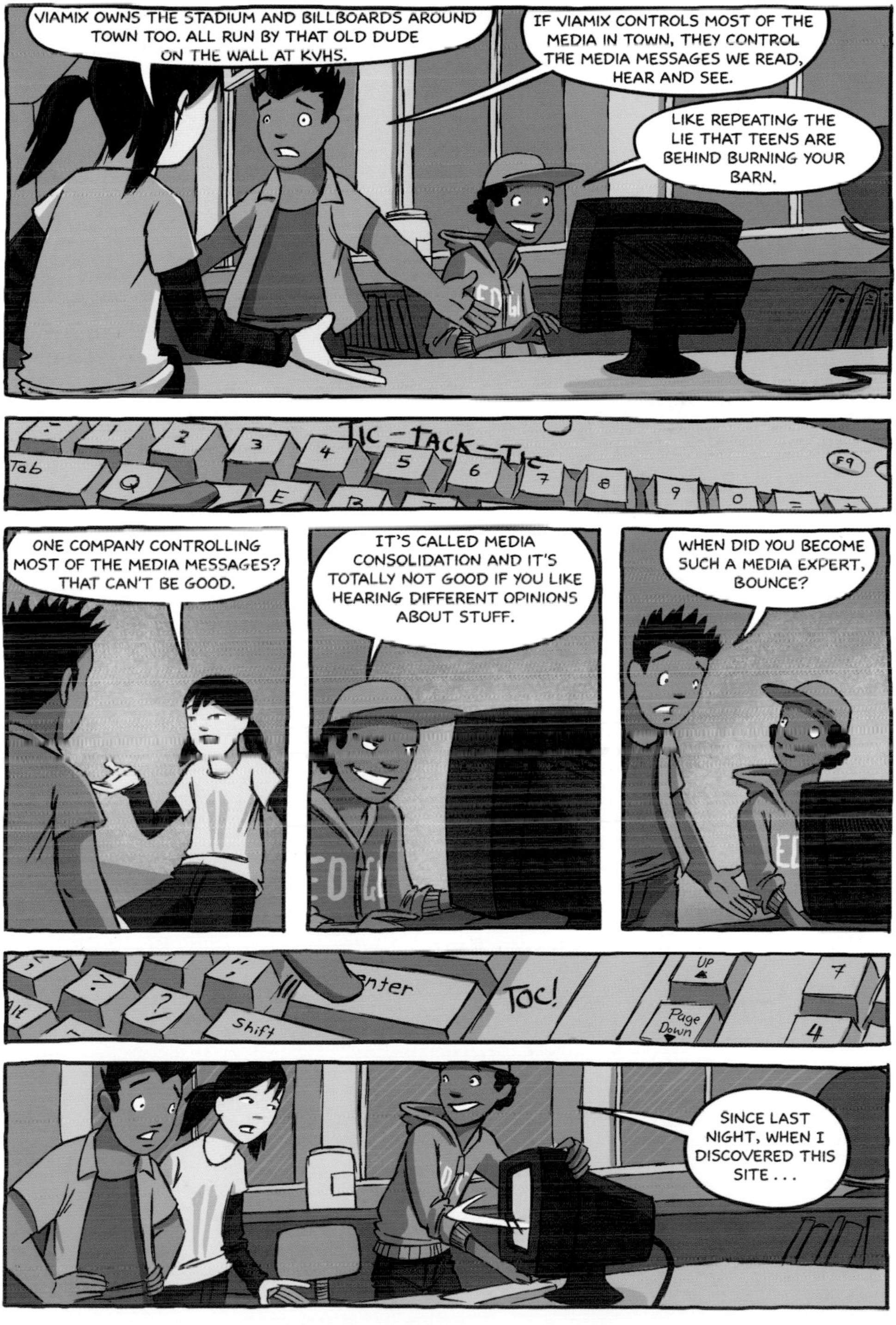
VIAMIX OWNS THE STADIUM AND BILLBOARDS AROUND TOWN TOO. ALL RUN BY THAT OLD DUDE ON THE WALL AT KVHS.
IF VIAMIX CONTROLS MOST OF THE MEDIA IN TOWN, THEY CONTROL THE MEDIA MESSAGES WE READ, HEAR AND SEE.
LIKE REPEATING THE LIE THAT TEENS ARE BEHIND BURNING YOUR BARN.
TIC-TACK-TIC
ONE COMPANY CONTROLLING MOST OF THE MEDIA MESSAGES? THAT CAN'T BE GOOD.
IT'S CALLED MEDIA CONSOLIDATION AND IT'S TOTALLY NOT GOOD IF YOU LIKE HEARING DIFFERENT OPINIONS ABOUT STUFF.
WHEN DID YOU BECOME SUCH A MEDIA EXPERT, BOUNCE?
TOC!
SINCE LAST NIGHT, WHEN I DISCOVERED THIS SITE . . .

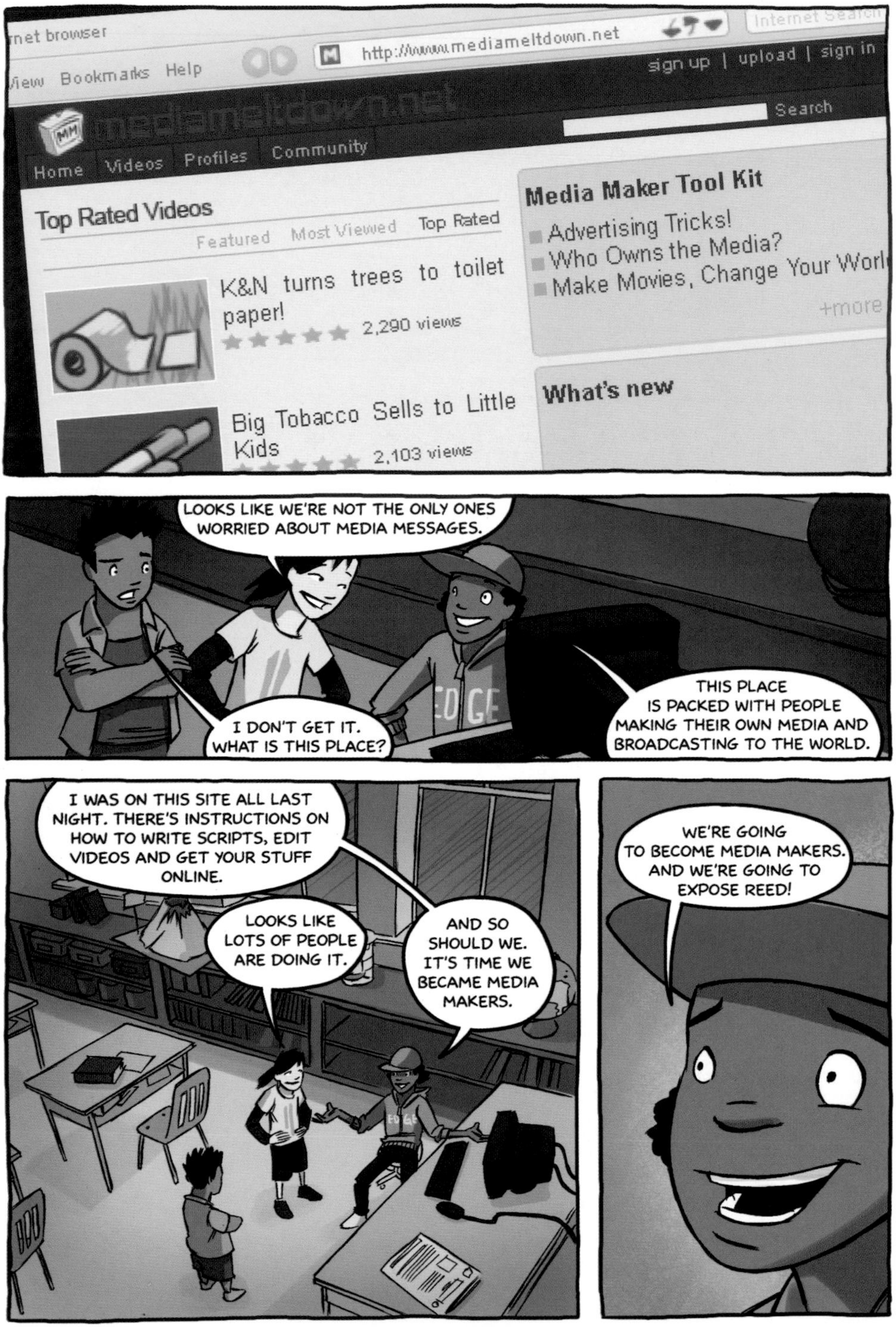
net browser
View Bookmarks Help
http://www.mediameltdown.net
sign up | upload | sign in
Internet Search
mediameltdown.net
Search
Home Videos Profiles Community
Top Rated Videos
Featured Most Viewed Top Rated
K&N turns trees to toilet paper!
2,290 views
Big Tobacco Sells to Little Kids
2,103 views
Media Maker Tool Kit
Advertising Tricks!
Who Owns the Media?
Make Movies, Change Your Worl
+more
What's new
LOOKS LIKE WE'RE NOT THE ONLY ONES WORRIED ABOUT MEDIA MESSAGES.
I DON'T GET IT. WHAT IS THIS PLACE?
THIS PLACE IS PACKED WITH PEOPLE MAKING THEIR OWN MEDIA AND BROADCASTING TO THE WORLD.
EDGE
I WAS ON THIS SITE ALL LAST NIGHT. THERE'S INSTRUCTIONS ON HOW TO WRITE SCRIPTS, EDIT VIDEOS AND GET YOUR STUFF ONLINE.
LOOKS LIKE LOTS OF PEOPLE ARE DOING IT.
AND SO SHOULD WE. IT'S TIME WE BECAME MEDIA MAKERS.
WE'RE GOING TO BECOME MEDIA MAKERS. AND WE'RE GOING TO EXPOSE REED!

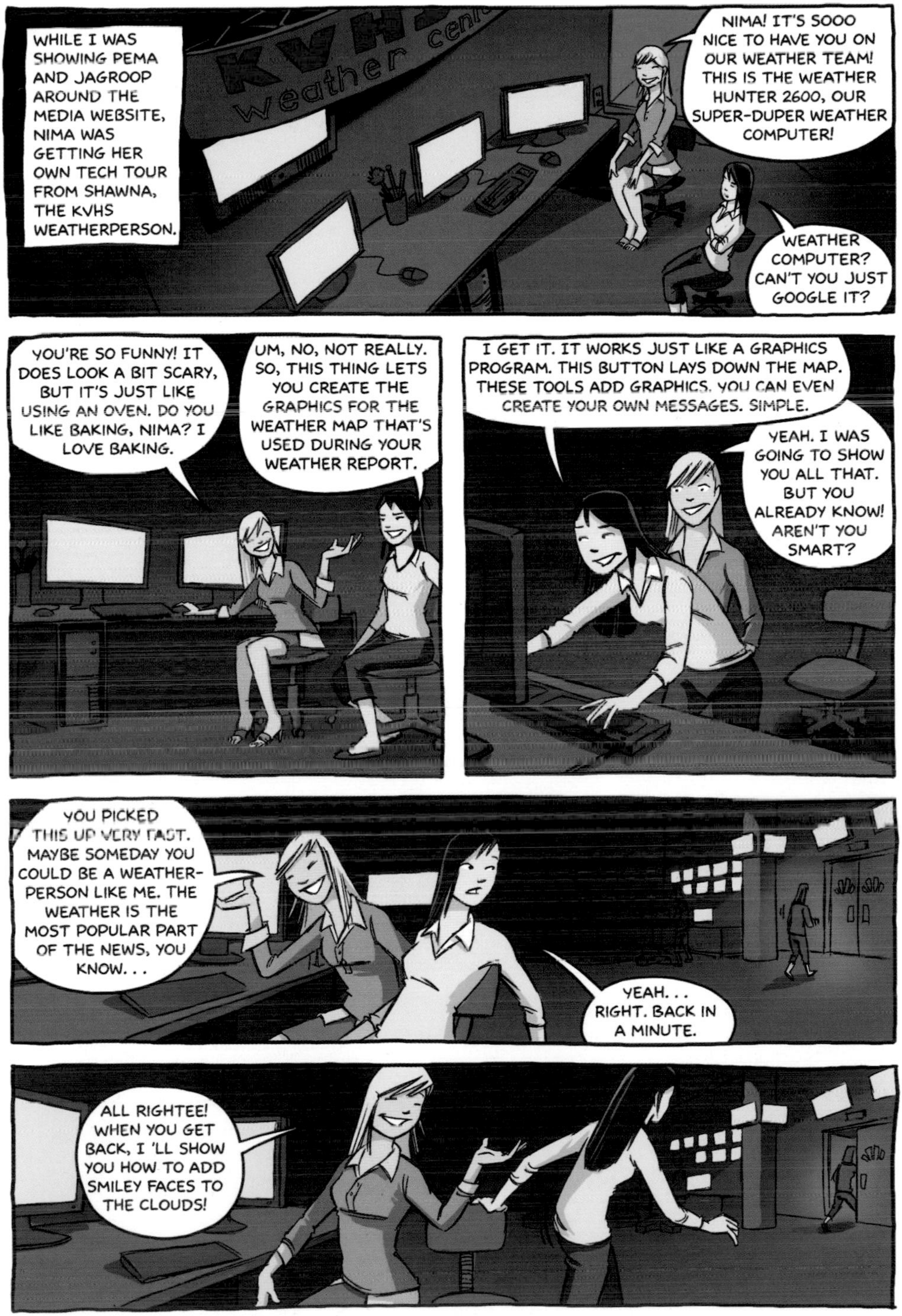
KVHS weather centre
WHILE I WAS SHOWING PEMA AND JAGROOP AROUND THE MEDIA WEBSITE, NIMA WAS GETTING HER OWN TECH TOUR FROM SHAWNA, THE KVHS WEATHERPERSON.
NIMA! IT'S SOOO NICE TO HAVE YOU ON OUR WEATHER TEAM! THIS IS THE WEATHER HUNTER 2600, OUR SUPER-DUPER WEATHER COMPUTER!
WEATHER COMPUTER? CAN'T YOU JUST GOOGLE IT?
YOU'RE SO FUNNY! IT DOES LOOK A BIT SCARY, BUT IT'S JUST LIKE USING AN OVEN. DO YOU LIKE BAKING, NIMA? I LOVE BAKING.
UM, NO, NOT REALLY. SO, THIS THING LETS YOU CREATE THE GRAPHICS FOR THE WEATHER MAP THAT'S USED DURING YOUR WEATHER REPORT.
I GET IT. IT WORKS JUST LIKE A GRAPHICS PROGRAM. THIS BUTTON LAYS DOWN THE MAP. THESE TOOLS ADD GRAPHICS. YOU CAN EVEN CREATE YOUR OWN MESSAGES. SIMPLE.
YEAH. I WAS GOING TO SHOW YOU ALL THAT. BUT YOU ALREADY KNOW! AREN'T YOU SMART?
YOU PICKED THIS UP VERY FAST. MAYBE SOMEDAY YOU COULD BE A WEATHER-PERSON LIKE ME. THE WEATHER IS THE MOST POPULAR PART OF THE NEWS, YOU KNOW. . .
YEAH. . . RIGHT. BACK IN A MINUTE.
ALL RIGHTEE! WHEN YOU GET BACK, I 'LL SHOW YOU HOW TO ADD SMILEY FACES TO THE CLOUDS!

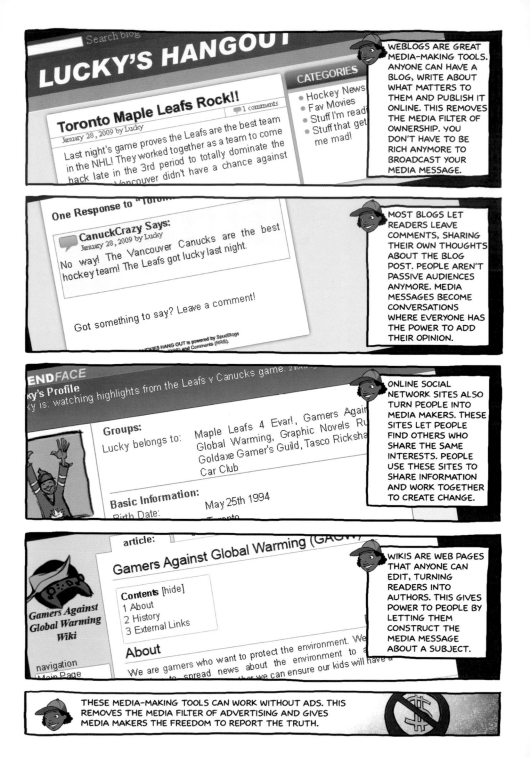

LUCKY'S HANGOUT

Search blog

WEBLOGS ARE GREAT MEDIA-MAKING TOOLS. ANYONE CAN HAVE A BLOG, WRITE ABOUT WHAT MATTERS TO THEM AND PUBLISH IT ONLINE. THIS REMOVES THE MEDIA FILTER OF OWNERSHIP. YOU DON'T HAVE TO BE RICH ANYMORE TO BROADCAST YOUR MEDIA MESSAGE.

Toronto Maple Leafs Rock!!

1 comments

January 28, 2009 by Lucky

Last night's game proves the Leafs are the best team in the NHL! They worked together as a team to come back late in the 3rd period to totally dominate the Vancouver didn't have a chance against

CATEGORIES
- Hockey News
- Fav Movies
- Stuff I'm readi
- Stuff that get me mad!

One Response to "Toro

MOST BLOGS LET READERS LEAVE COMMENTS, SHARING THEIR OWN THOUGHTS ABOUT THE BLOG POST. PEOPLE AREN'T PASSIVE AUDIENCES ANYMORE. MEDIA MESSAGES BECOME CONVERSATIONS WHERE EVERYONE HAS THE POWER TO ADD THEIR OPINION.

CanuckCrazy Says:
January 28, 2009 by Lucky

No way! The Vancouver Canucks are the best hockey team! The Leafs got lucky last night.

Got something to say? Leave a comment!

LUCKIES HANG OUT is powered by SpudBlogs
and Comments (RRS).

ENDFACE

ky's Profile
ky is: watching highlights from the Leafs v Canucks game.

ONLINE SOCIAL NETWORK SITES ALSO TURN PEOPLE INTO MEDIA MAKERS. THESE SITES LET PEOPLE FIND OTHERS WHO SHARE THE SAME INTERESTS. PEOPLE USE THESE SITES TO SHARE INFORMATION AND WORK TOGETHER TO CREATE CHANGE.

Groups:
Lucky belongs to: Maple Leafs 4 Evar!, Gamers Again Global Warming, Graphic Novels Ru Goldaxe Gamer's Guild, Tasco Ricksha Car Club

Basic Information:
Birth Date: May 25th 1994

---

article:

Gamers Against Global Warming (GAGW)

WIKIS ARE WEB PAGES THAT ANYONE CAN EDIT, TURNING READERS INTO AUTHORS. THIS GIVES POWER TO PEOPLE BY LETTING THEM CONSTRUCT THE MEDIA MESSAGE ABOUT A SUBJECT.

Gamers Against Global Warming Wiki

Contents [hide]
1 About
2 History
3 External Links

About

We are gamers who want to protect the environment. We to spread news about the environment to a er we can ensure our kids will have a

navigation
Main Page

THESE MEDIA-MAKING TOOLS CAN WORK WITHOUT ADS. THIS REMOVES THE MEDIA FILTER OF ADVERTISING AND GIVES MEDIA MAKERS THE FREEDOM TO REPORT THE TRUTH.

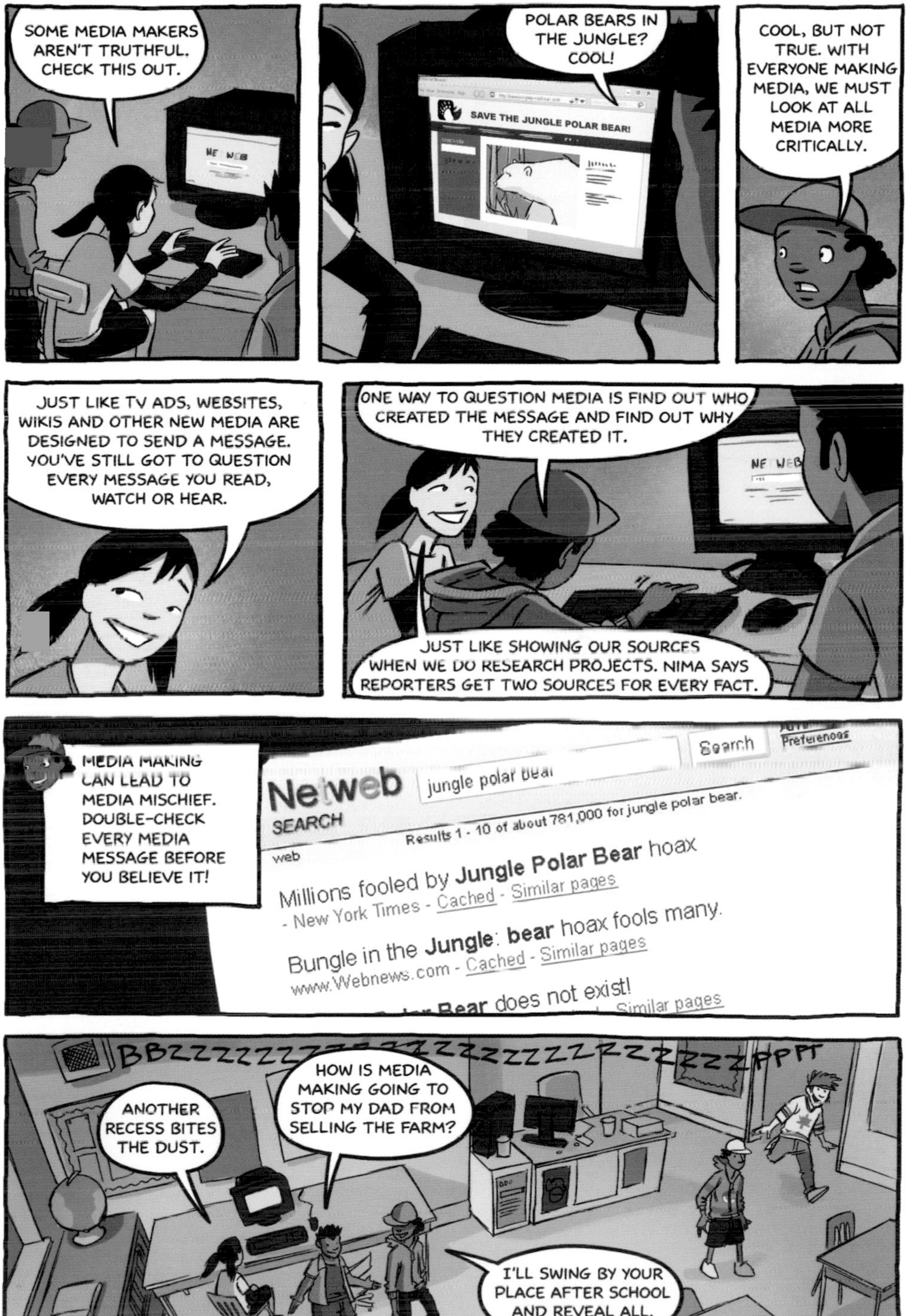
SOME MEDIA MAKERS AREN'T TRUTHFUL. CHECK THIS OUT.
POLAR BEARS IN THE JUNGLE? COOL!
SAVE THE JUNGLE POLAR BEAR!
COOL, BUT NOT TRUE. WITH EVERYONE MAKING MEDIA, WE MUST LOOK AT ALL MEDIA MORE CRITICALLY.
JUST LIKE TV ADS, WEBSITES, WIKIS AND OTHER NEW MEDIA ARE DESIGNED TO SEND A MESSAGE. YOU'VE STILL GOT TO QUESTION EVERY MESSAGE YOU READ, WATCH OR HEAR.
ONE WAY TO QUESTION MEDIA IS FIND OUT WHO CREATED THE MESSAGE AND FIND OUT WHY THEY CREATED IT.
JUST LIKE SHOWING OUR SOURCES WHEN WE DO RESEARCH PROJECTS. NIMA SAYS REPORTERS GET TWO SOURCES FOR EVERY FACT.
MEDIA MAKING CAN LEAD TO MEDIA MISCHIEF. DOUBLE-CHECK EVERY MEDIA MESSAGE BEFORE YOU BELIEVE IT!
Netweb SEARCH
jungle polar bear
Search
Preferences
Results 1 - 10 of about 781,000 for jungle polar bear.
web
Millions fooled by Jungle Polar Bear hoax
- New York Times - Cached - Similar pages
Bungle in the Jungle: bear hoax fools many.
www.Webnews.com - Cached - Similar pages
Bear does not exist!
Similar pages
BBZZZZZZZZZZZZZZZZZZZZZZZZZPPPT
ANOTHER RECESS BITES THE DUST.
HOW IS MEDIA MAKING GOING TO STOP MY DAD FROM SELLING THE FARM?
I'LL SWING BY YOUR PLACE AFTER SCHOOL AND REVEAL ALL.

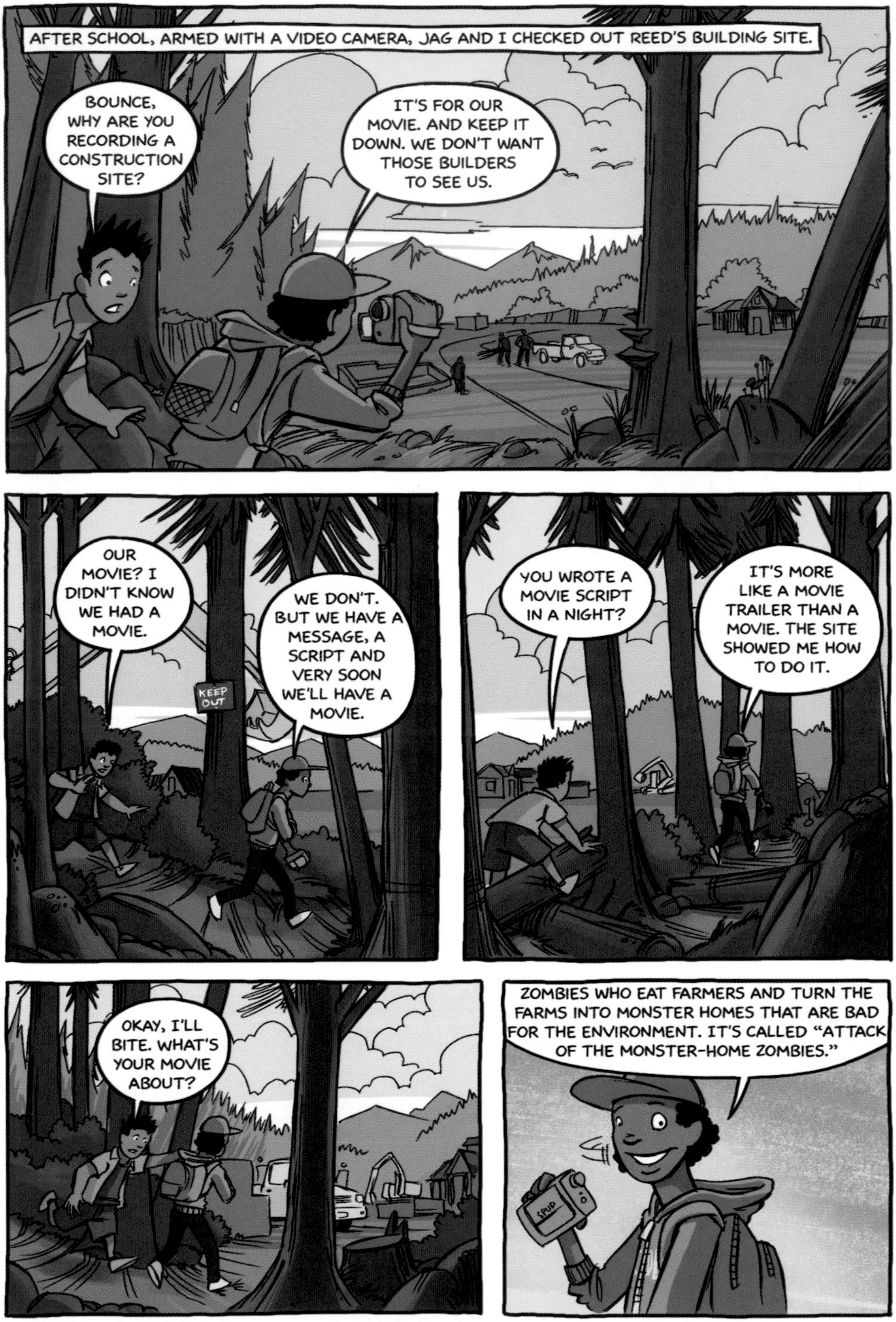
AFTER SCHOOL, ARMED WITH A VIDEO CAMERA, JAG AND I CHECKED OUT REED'S BUILDING SITE.
BOUNCE, WHY ARE YOU RECORDING A CONSTRUCTION SITE?
IT'S FOR OUR MOVIE. AND KEEP IT DOWN. WE DON'T WANT THOSE BUILDERS TO SEE US.
OUR MOVIE? I DIDN'T KNOW WE HAD A MOVIE.
KEEP OUT
WE DON'T. BUT WE HAVE A MESSAGE, A SCRIPT AND VERY SOON WE'LL HAVE A MOVIE.
YOU WROTE A MOVIE SCRIPT IN A NIGHT?
IT'S MORE LIKE A MOVIE TRAILER THAN A MOVIE. THE SITE SHOWED ME HOW TO DO IT.
OKAY, I'LL BITE. WHAT'S YOUR MOVIE ABOUT?
ZOMBIES WHO EAT FARMERS AND TURN THE FARMS INTO MONSTER HOMES THAT ARE BAD FOR THE ENVIRONMENT. IT'S CALLED "ATTACK OF THE MONSTER-HOME ZOMBIES."
SPUD

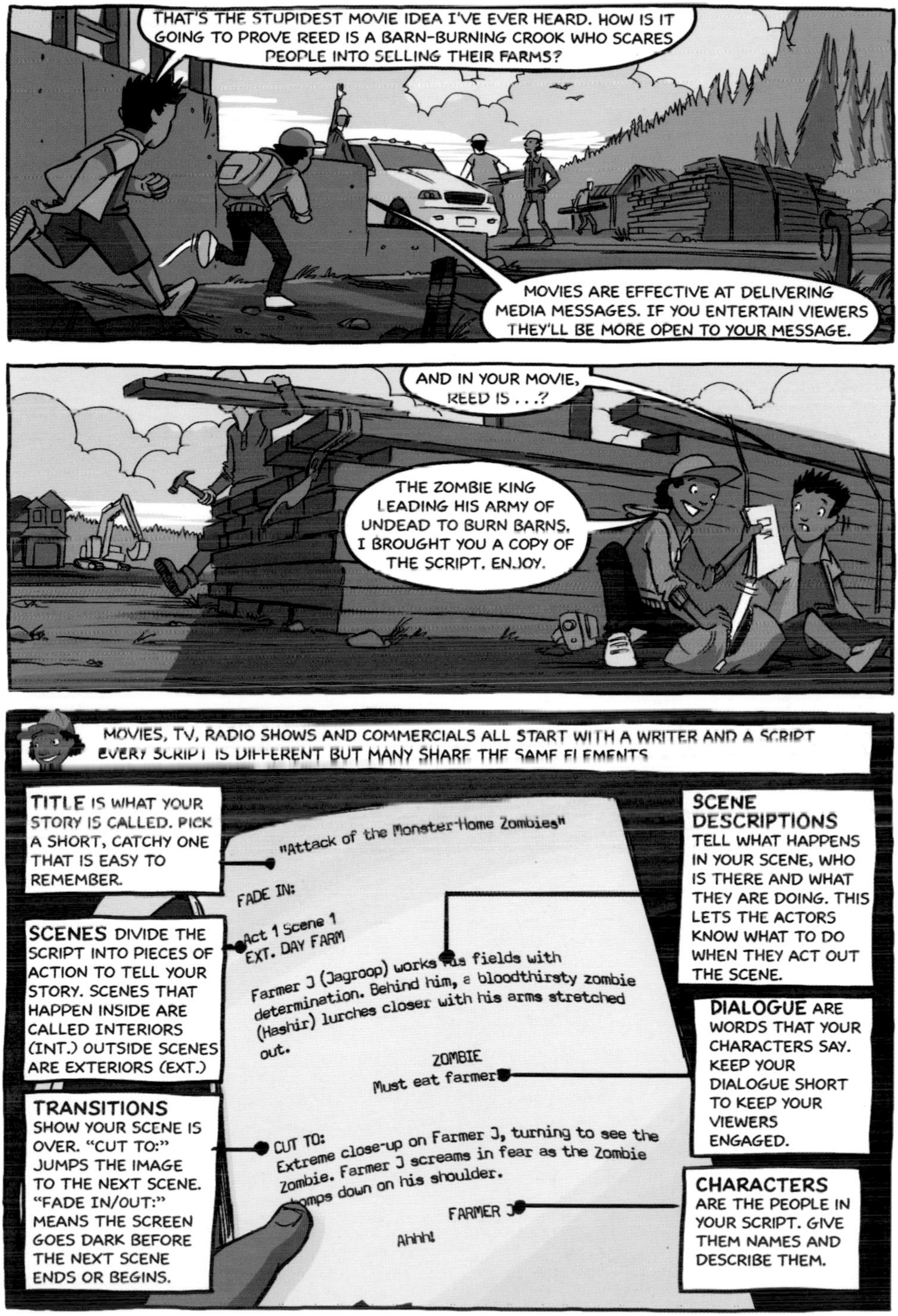
THAT'S THE STUPIDEST MOVIE IDEA I'VE EVER HEARD. HOW IS IT GOING TO PROVE REED IS A BARN-BURNING CROOK WHO SCARES PEOPLE INTO SELLING THEIR FARMS?
MOVIES ARE EFFECTIVE AT DELIVERING MEDIA MESSAGES. IF YOU ENTERTAIN VIEWERS THEY'LL BE MORE OPEN TO YOUR MESSAGE.
AND IN YOUR MOVIE, REED IS . . .?
THE ZOMBIE KING LEADING HIS ARMY OF UNDEAD TO BURN BARNS. I BROUGHT YOU A COPY OF THE SCRIPT. ENJOY.
MOVIES, TV, RADIO SHOWS AND COMMERCIALS ALL START WITH A WRITER AND A SCRIPT. EVERY SCRIPT IS DIFFERENT BUT MANY SHARE THE SAME ELEMENTS.
TITLE IS WHAT YOUR STORY IS CALLED. PICK A SHORT, CATCHY ONE THAT IS EASY TO REMEMBER.
SCENES DIVIDE THE SCRIPT INTO PIECES OF ACTION TO TELL YOUR STORY. SCENES THAT HAPPEN INSIDE ARE CALLED INTERIORS (INT.) OUTSIDE SCENES ARE EXTERIORS (EXT.)
TRANSITIONS SHOW YOUR SCENE IS OVER. "CUT TO:" JUMPS THE IMAGE TO THE NEXT SCENE. "FADE IN/OUT:" MEANS THE SCREEN GOES DARK BEFORE THE NEXT SCENE ENDS OR BEGINS.
"Attack of the Monster-Home Zombies"
FADE IN:
Act 1 Scene 1
EXT. DAY FARM
Farmer J (Jagroop) works his fields with determination. Behind him, a bloodthirsty zombie (Hashir) lurches closer with his arms stretched out.
ZOMBIE
Must eat farmer!
CUT TO:
Extreme close-up on Farmer J, turning to see the Zombie. Farmer J screams in fear as the Zombie chomps down on his shoulder.
FARMER J
Ahhh!
SCENE DESCRIPTIONS TELL WHAT HAPPENS IN YOUR SCENE, WHO IS THERE AND WHAT THEY ARE DOING. THIS LETS THE ACTORS KNOW WHAT TO DO WHEN THEY ACT OUT THE SCENE.
DIALOGUE ARE WORDS THAT YOUR CHARACTERS SAY. KEEP YOUR DIALOGUE SHORT TO KEEP YOUR VIEWERS ENGAGED.
CHARACTERS ARE THE PEOPLE IN YOUR SCRIPT. GIVE THEM NAMES AND DESCRIBE THEM.

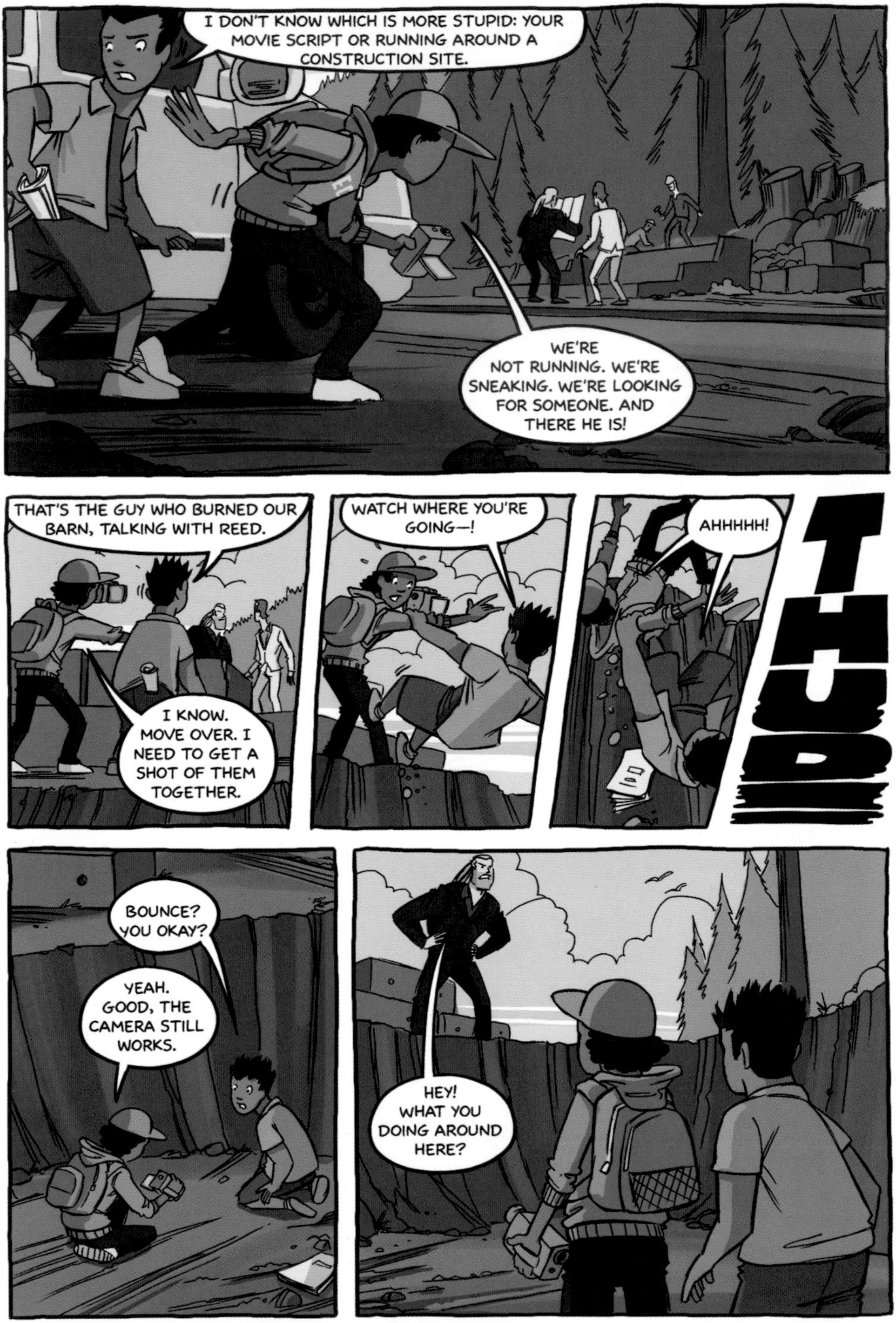
I DON'T KNOW WHICH IS MORE STUPID: YOUR MOVIE SCRIPT OR RUNNING AROUND A CONSTRUCTION SITE.
WE'RE NOT RUNNING. WE'RE SNEAKING. WE'RE LOOKING FOR SOMEONE. AND THERE HE IS!
THAT'S THE GUY WHO BURNED OUR BARN, TALKING WITH REED.
I KNOW. MOVE OVER. I NEED TO GET A SHOT OF THEM TOGETHER.
WATCH WHERE YOU'RE GOING—!
AHHHHH!
THUD
BOUNCE? YOU OKAY?
YEAH. GOOD, THE CAMERA STILL WORKS.
HEY! WHAT YOU DOING AROUND HERE?

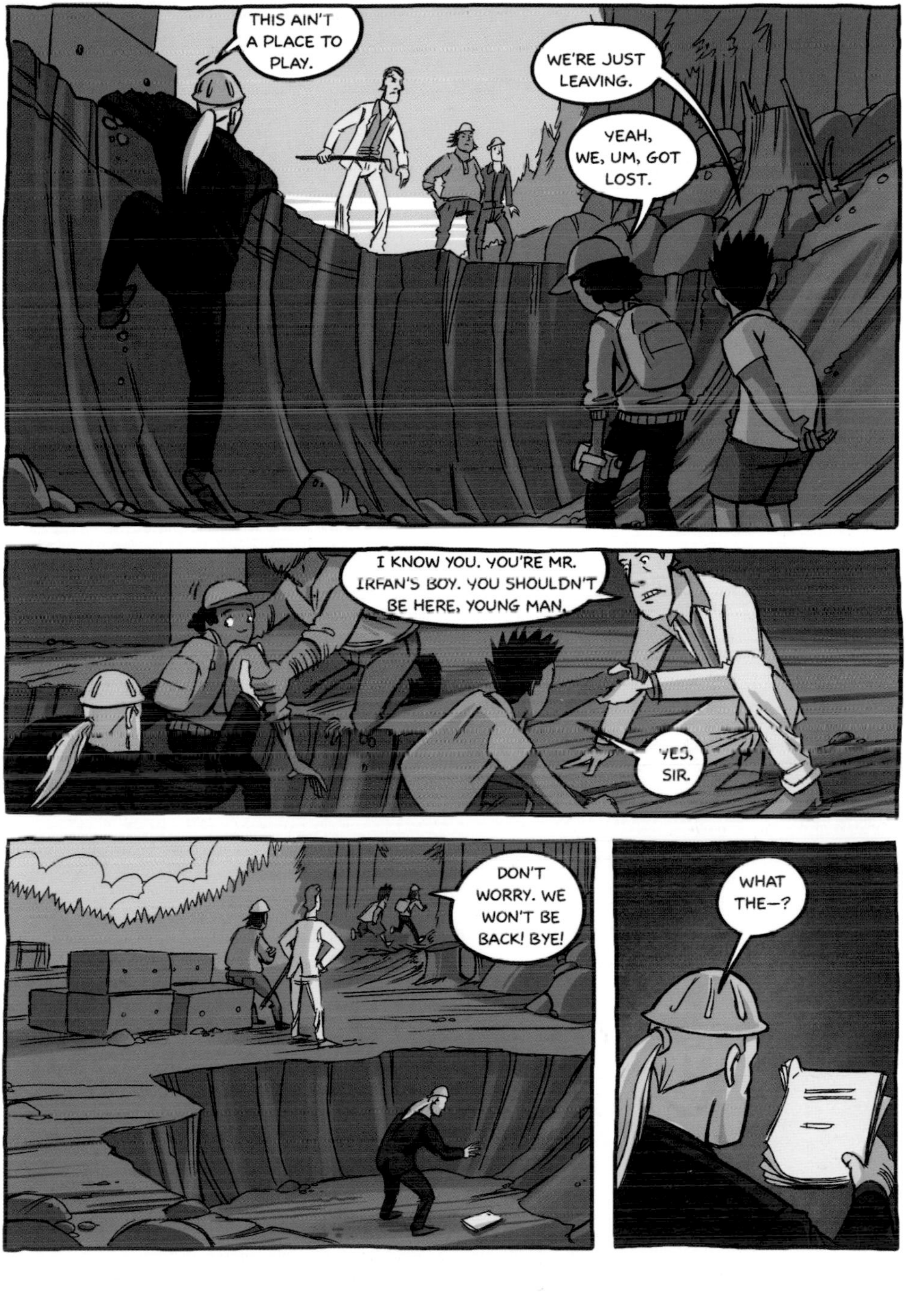
THIS AIN'T A PLACE TO PLAY.
WE'RE JUST LEAVING.
YEAH, WE, UM, GOT LOST.
I KNOW YOU. YOU'RE MR. IRFAN'S BOY. YOU SHOULDN'T BE HERE, YOUNG MAN.
YES, SIR.
DON'T WORRY. WE WON'T BE BACK! BYE!
WHAT THE—?

CHAPTER 5

ZOMBIES AND SECRET MEETINGS

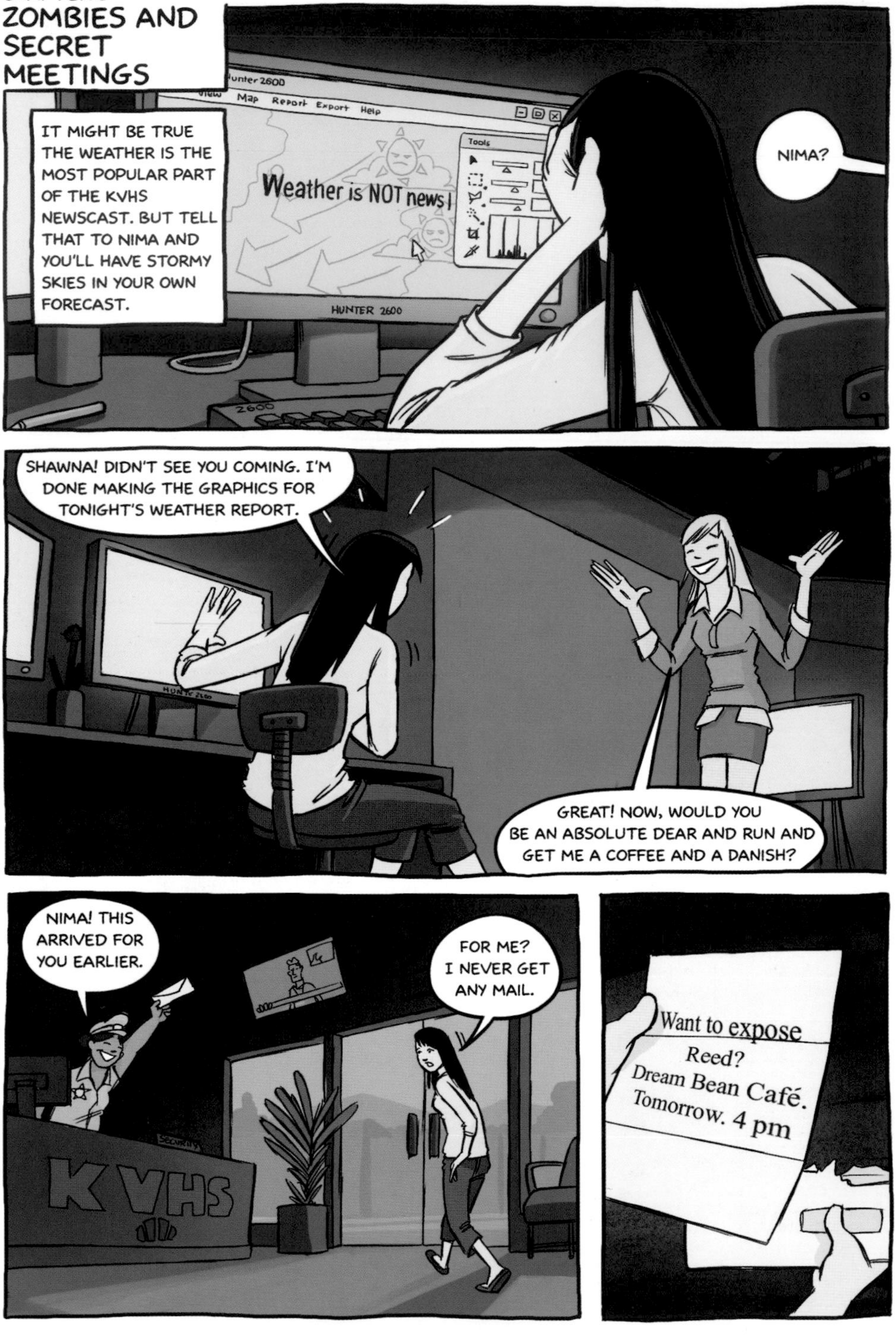

IT MIGHT BE TRUE THE WEATHER IS THE MOST POPULAR PART OF THE KVHS NEWSCAST. BUT TELL THAT TO NIMA AND YOU'LL HAVE STORMY SKIES IN YOUR OWN FORECAST.
Hunter 2600
Map Report Export Help
Tools
Weather is NOT news!
HUNTER 2600
NIMA?
SHAWNA! DIDN'T SEE YOU COMING. I'M DONE MAKING THE GRAPHICS FOR TONIGHT'S WEATHER REPORT.
GREAT! NOW, WOULD YOU BE AN ABSOLUTE DEAR AND RUN AND GET ME A COFFEE AND A DANISH?
NIMA! THIS ARRIVED FOR YOU EARLIER.
FOR ME? I NEVER GET ANY MAIL.
SECURITY
KVHS
Want to expose Reed? Dream Bean Café. Tomorrow. 4 pm

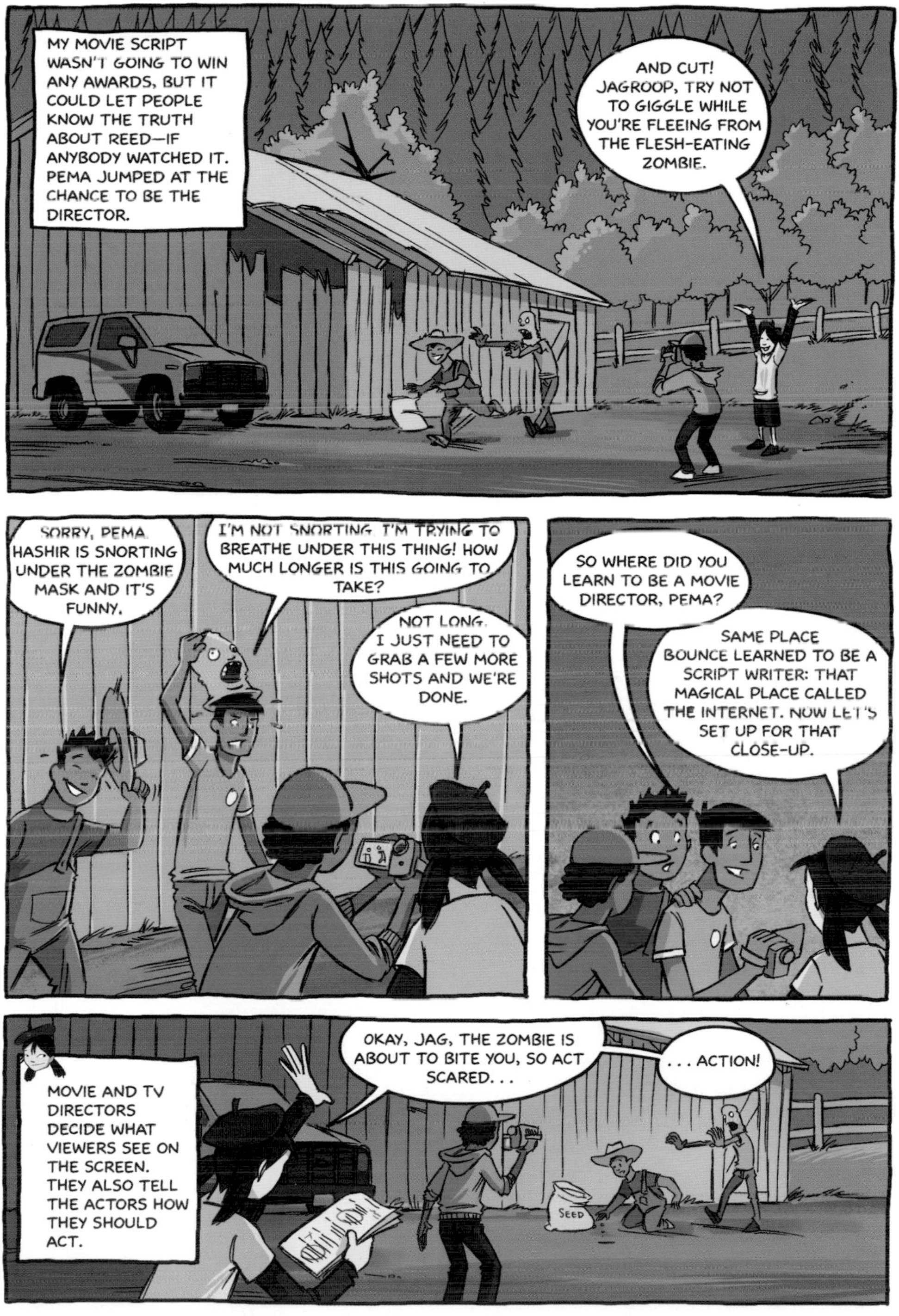
MY MOVIE SCRIPT WASN'T GOING TO WIN ANY AWARDS, BUT IT COULD LET PEOPLE KNOW THE TRUTH ABOUT REED—IF ANYBODY WATCHED IT. PEMA JUMPED AT THE CHANCE TO BE THE DIRECTOR.
AND CUT! JAGROOP, TRY NOT TO GIGGLE WHILE YOU'RE FLEEING FROM THE FLESH-EATING ZOMBIE.
SORRY, PEMA. HASHIR IS SNORTING UNDER THE ZOMBIE MASK AND IT'S FUNNY.
I'M NOT SNORTING. I'M TRYING TO BREATHE UNDER THIS THING! HOW MUCH LONGER IS THIS GOING TO TAKE?
NOT LONG. I JUST NEED TO GRAB A FEW MORE SHOTS AND WE'RE DONE.
SO WHERE DID YOU LEARN TO BE A MOVIE DIRECTOR, PEMA?
SAME PLACE BOUNCE LEARNED TO BE A SCRIPT WRITER: THAT MAGICAL PLACE CALLED THE INTERNET. NOW LET'S SET UP FOR THAT CLOSE-UP.
MOVIE AND TV DIRECTORS DECIDE WHAT VIEWERS SEE ON THE SCREEN. THEY ALSO TELL THE ACTORS HOW THEY SHOULD ACT.
OKAY, JAG, THE ZOMBIE IS ABOUT TO BITE YOU, SO ACT SCARED. . .
. . . ACTION!
SEED

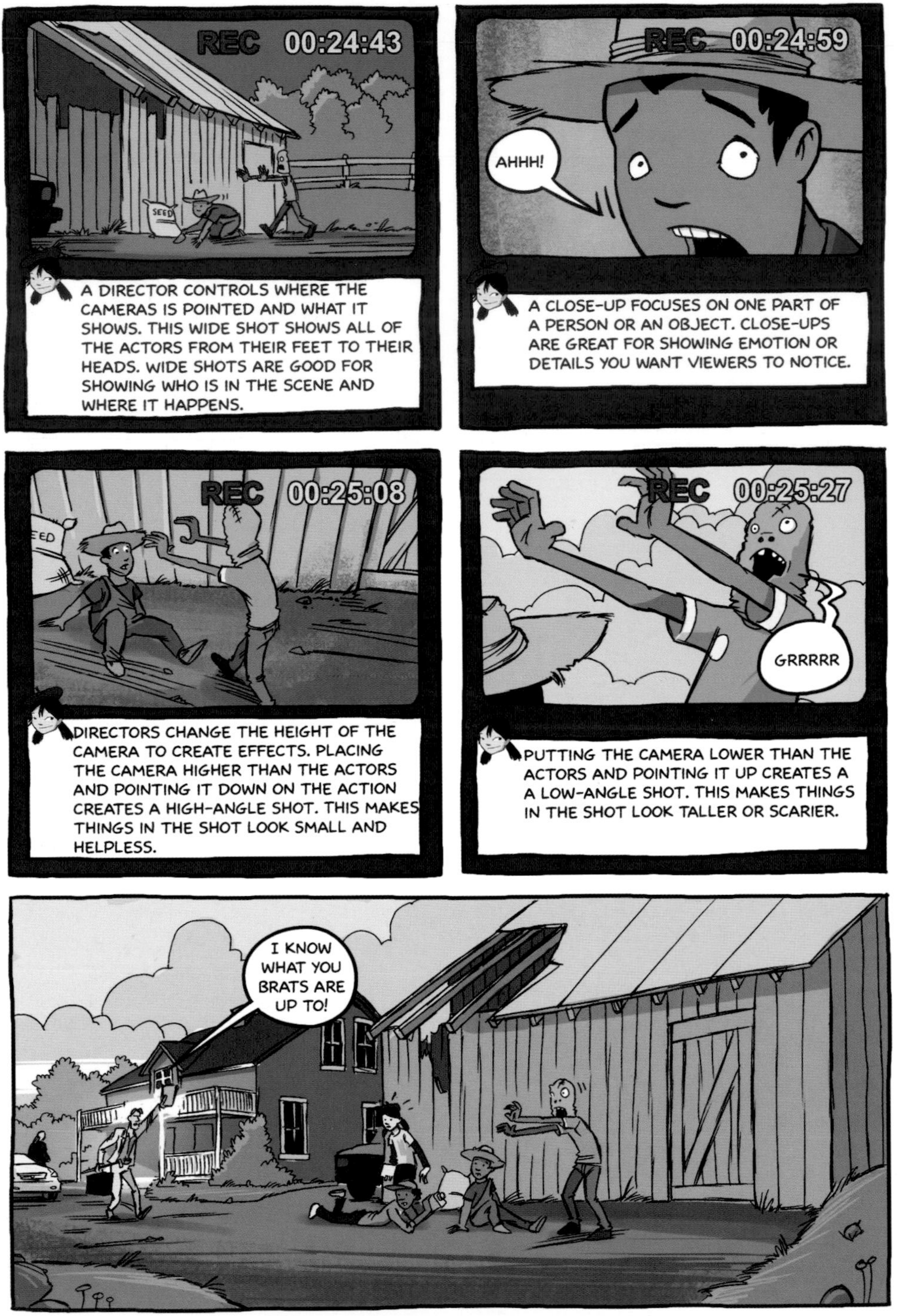
REC 00:24:43
SEED
A DIRECTOR CONTROLS WHERE THE CAMERAS IS POINTED AND WHAT IT SHOWS. THIS WIDE SHOT SHOWS ALL OF THE ACTORS FROM THEIR FEET TO THEIR HEADS. WIDE SHOTS ARE GOOD FOR SHOWING WHO IS IN THE SCENE AND WHERE IT HAPPENS.
REC 00:24:59
AHHH!
A CLOSE-UP FOCUSES ON ONE PART OF A PERSON OR AN OBJECT. CLOSE-UPS ARE GREAT FOR SHOWING EMOTION OR DETAILS YOU WANT VIEWERS TO NOTICE.
REC 00:25:08
EED
DIRECTORS CHANGE THE HEIGHT OF THE CAMERA TO CREATE EFFECTS. PLACING THE CAMERA HIGHER THAN THE ACTORS AND POINTING IT DOWN ON THE ACTION CREATES A HIGH-ANGLE SHOT. THIS MAKES THINGS IN THE SHOT LOOK SMALL AND HELPLESS.
REC 00:25:27
GRRRRR
PUTTING THE CAMERA LOWER THAN THE ACTORS AND POINTING IT UP CREATES A A LOW-ANGLE SHOT. THIS MAKES THINGS IN THE SHOT LOOK TALLER OR SCARIER.
I KNOW WHAT YOU BRATS ARE UP TO!

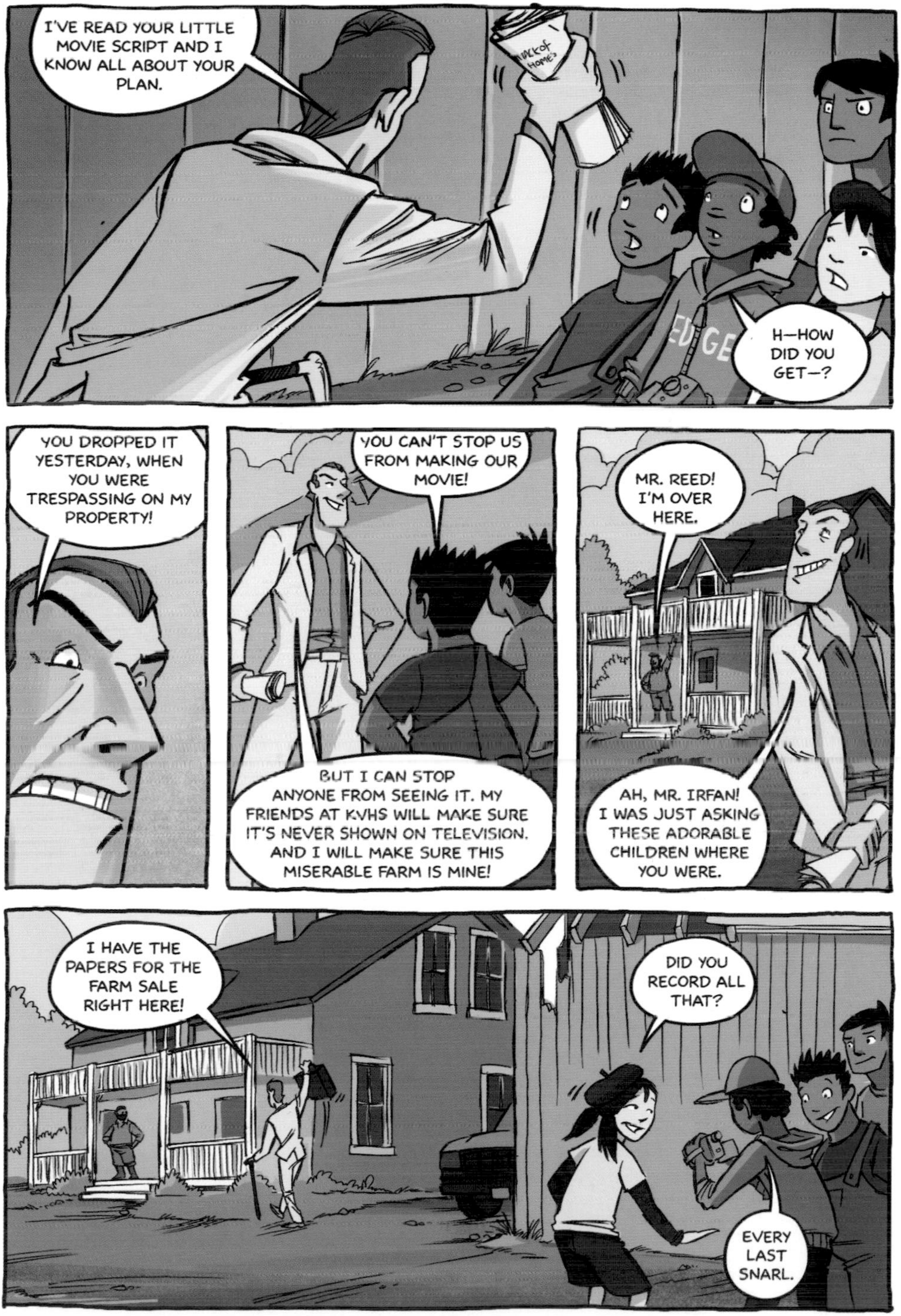
I'VE READ YOUR LITTLE MOVIE SCRIPT AND I KNOW ALL ABOUT YOUR PLAN.
H—HOW DID YOU GET—?
YOU DROPPED IT YESTERDAY, WHEN YOU WERE TRESPASSING ON MY PROPERTY!
YOU CAN'T STOP US FROM MAKING OUR MOVIE!
BUT I CAN STOP ANYONE FROM SEEING IT. MY FRIENDS AT KVHS WILL MAKE SURE IT'S NEVER SHOWN ON TELEVISION. AND I WILL MAKE SURE THIS MISERABLE FARM IS MINE!
MR. REED! I'M OVER HERE.
AH, MR. IRFAN! I WAS JUST ASKING THESE ADORABLE CHILDREN WHERE YOU WERE.
I HAVE THE PAPERS FOR THE FARM SALE RIGHT HERE!
DID YOU RECORD ALL THAT?
EVERY LAST SNARL.

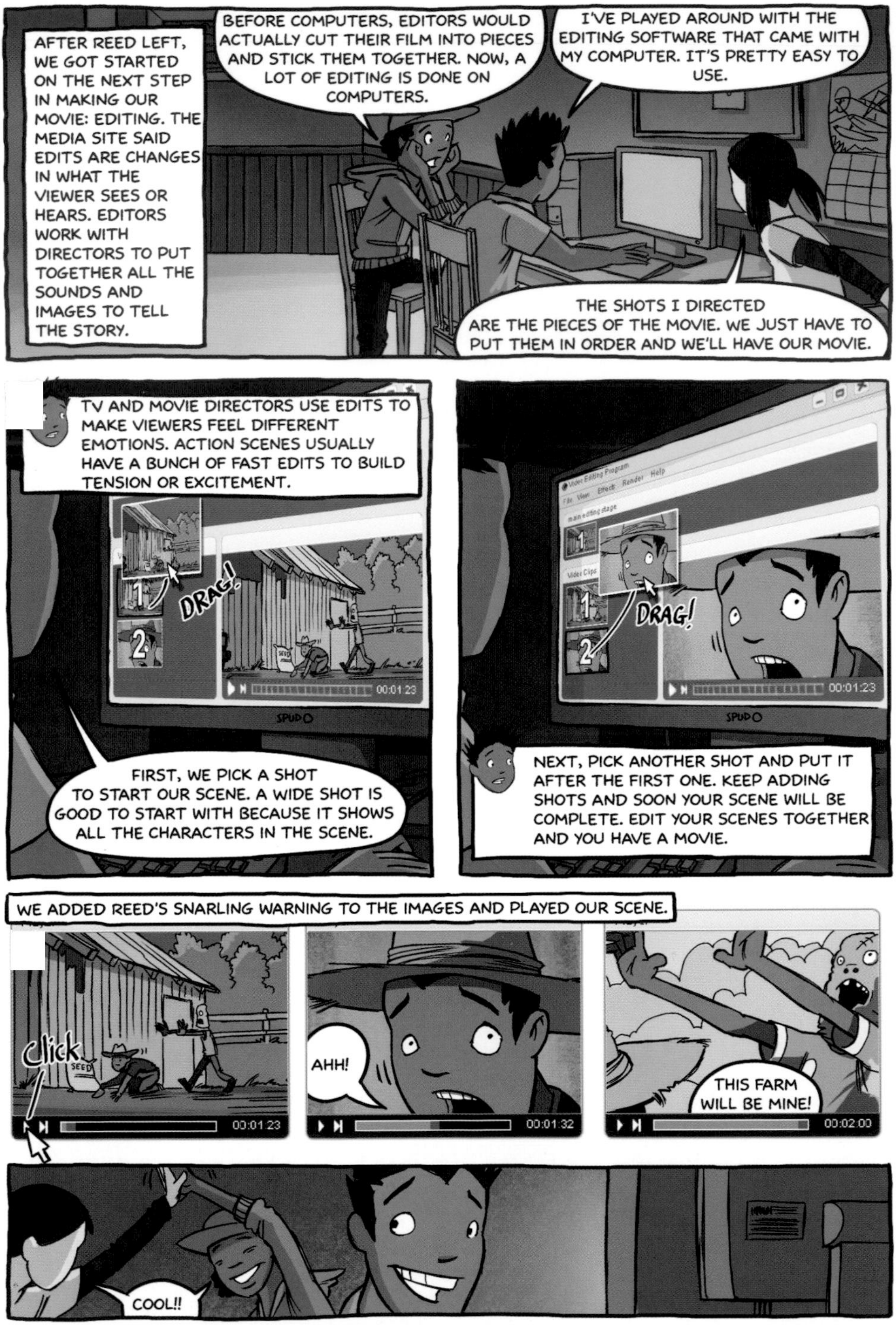
AFTER REED LEFT, WE GOT STARTED ON THE NEXT STEP IN MAKING OUR MOVIE: EDITING. THE MEDIA SITE SAID EDITS ARE CHANGES IN WHAT THE VIEWER SEES OR HEARS. EDITORS WORK WITH DIRECTORS TO PUT TOGETHER ALL THE SOUNDS AND IMAGES TO TELL THE STORY.
BEFORE COMPUTERS, EDITORS WOULD ACTUALLY CUT THEIR FILM INTO PIECES AND STICK THEM TOGETHER. NOW, A LOT OF EDITING IS DONE ON COMPUTERS.
I'VE PLAYED AROUND WITH THE EDITING SOFTWARE THAT CAME WITH MY COMPUTER. IT'S PRETTY EASY TO USE.
THE SHOTS I DIRECTED ARE THE PIECES OF THE MOVIE. WE JUST HAVE TO PUT THEM IN ORDER AND WE'LL HAVE OUR MOVIE.
TV AND MOVIE DIRECTORS USE EDITS TO MAKE VIEWERS FEEL DIFFERENT EMOTIONS. ACTION SCENES USUALLY HAVE A BUNCH OF FAST EDITS TO BUILD TENSION OR EXCITEMENT.
DRAG!
00:01:23
SPUDO
FIRST, WE PICK A SHOT TO START OUR SCENE. A WIDE SHOT IS GOOD TO START WITH BECAUSE IT SHOWS ALL THE CHARACTERS IN THE SCENE.
Video Editing Program
File View Effect Render Help
DRAG!
00:01:23
SPUDO
NEXT, PICK ANOTHER SHOT AND PUT IT AFTER THE FIRST ONE. KEEP ADDING SHOTS AND SOON YOUR SCENE WILL BE COMPLETE. EDIT YOUR SCENES TOGETHER AND YOU HAVE A MOVIE.
WE ADDED REED'S SNARLING WARNING TO THE IMAGES AND PLAYED OUR SCENE.
Click
SEED
00:01:23
AHH!
00:01:32
THIS FARM WILL BE MINE!
00:02:00
COOL!!

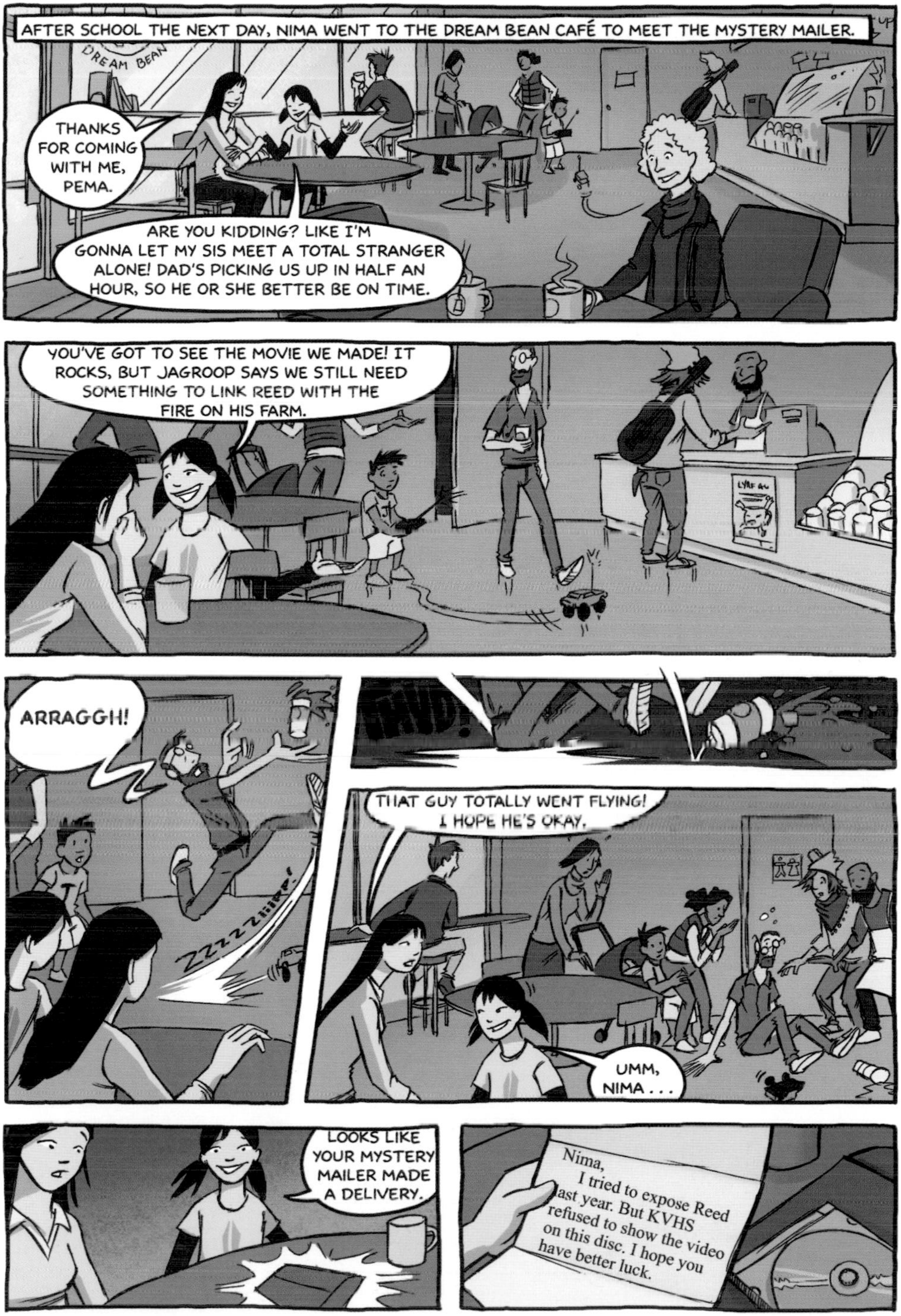
AFTER SCHOOL THE NEXT DAY, NIMA WENT TO THE DREAM BEAN CAFÉ TO MEET THE MYSTERY MAILER.
DREAM BEAN
THANKS FOR COMING WITH ME, PEMA.
ARE YOU KIDDING? LIKE I'M GONNA LET MY SIS MEET A TOTAL STRANGER ALONE! DAD'S PICKING US UP IN HALF AN HOUR, SO HE OR SHE BETTER BE ON TIME.
YOU'VE GOT TO SEE THE MOVIE WE MADE! IT ROCKS, BUT JAGROOP SAYS WE STILL NEED SOMETHING TO LINK REED WITH THE FIRE ON HIS FARM.
ARRAGGH!
ZZZZZIIIRP!
THUD!
THAT GUY TOTALLY WENT FLYING! I HOPE HE'S OKAY.
UMM, NIMA . . .
LOOKS LIKE YOUR MYSTERY MAILER MADE A DELIVERY.
Nima,
I tried to expose Reed last year. But KVHS refused to show the video on this disc. I hope you have better luck.

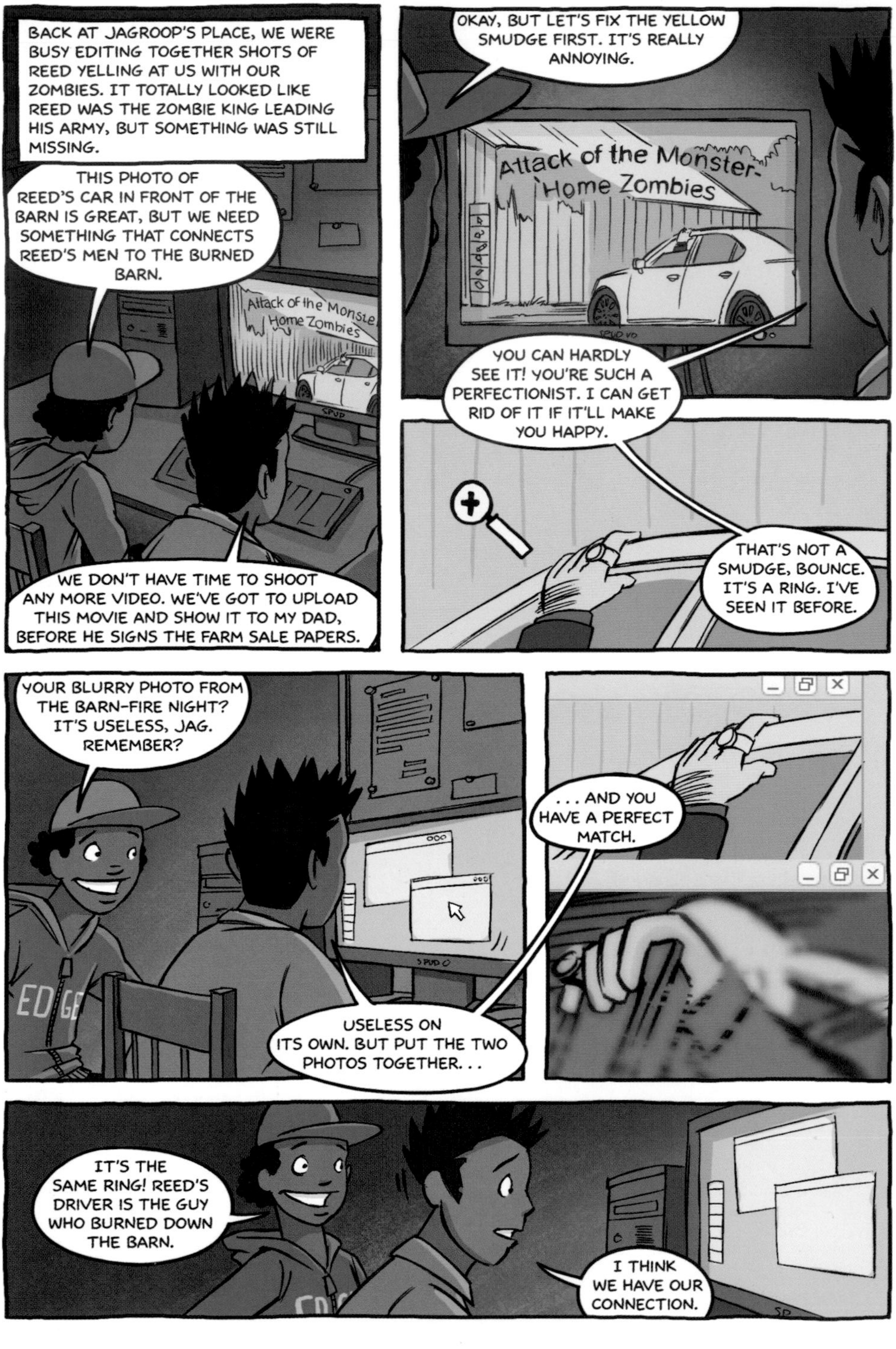

BACK AT JAGROOP'S PLACE, WE WERE BUSY EDITING TOGETHER SHOTS OF REED YELLING AT US WITH OUR ZOMBIES. IT TOTALLY LOOKED LIKE REED WAS THE ZOMBIE KING LEADING HIS ARMY, BUT SOMETHING WAS STILL MISSING.
THIS PHOTO OF REED'S CAR IN FRONT OF THE BARN IS GREAT, BUT WE NEED SOMETHING THAT CONNECTS REED'S MEN TO THE BURNED BARN.
Attack of the Monster Home Zombies
WE DON'T HAVE TIME TO SHOOT ANY MORE VIDEO. WE'VE GOT TO UPLOAD THIS MOVIE AND SHOW IT TO MY DAD, BEFORE HE SIGNS THE FARM SALE PAPERS.
OKAY, BUT LET'S FIX THE YELLOW SMUDGE FIRST. IT'S REALLY ANNOYING.
Attack of the Monster-Home Zombies
YOU CAN HARDLY SEE IT! YOU'RE SUCH A PERFECTIONIST. I CAN GET RID OF IT IF IT'LL MAKE YOU HAPPY.
THAT'S NOT A SMUDGE, BOUNCE. IT'S A RING. I'VE SEEN IT BEFORE.
YOUR BLURRY PHOTO FROM THE BARN-FIRE NIGHT? IT'S USELESS, JAG. REMEMBER?
USELESS ON ITS OWN. BUT PUT THE TWO PHOTOS TOGETHER. . .
. . . AND YOU HAVE A PERFECT MATCH.
IT'S THE SAME RING! REED'S DRIVER IS THE GUY WHO BURNED DOWN THE BARN.
I THINK WE HAVE OUR CONNECTION.

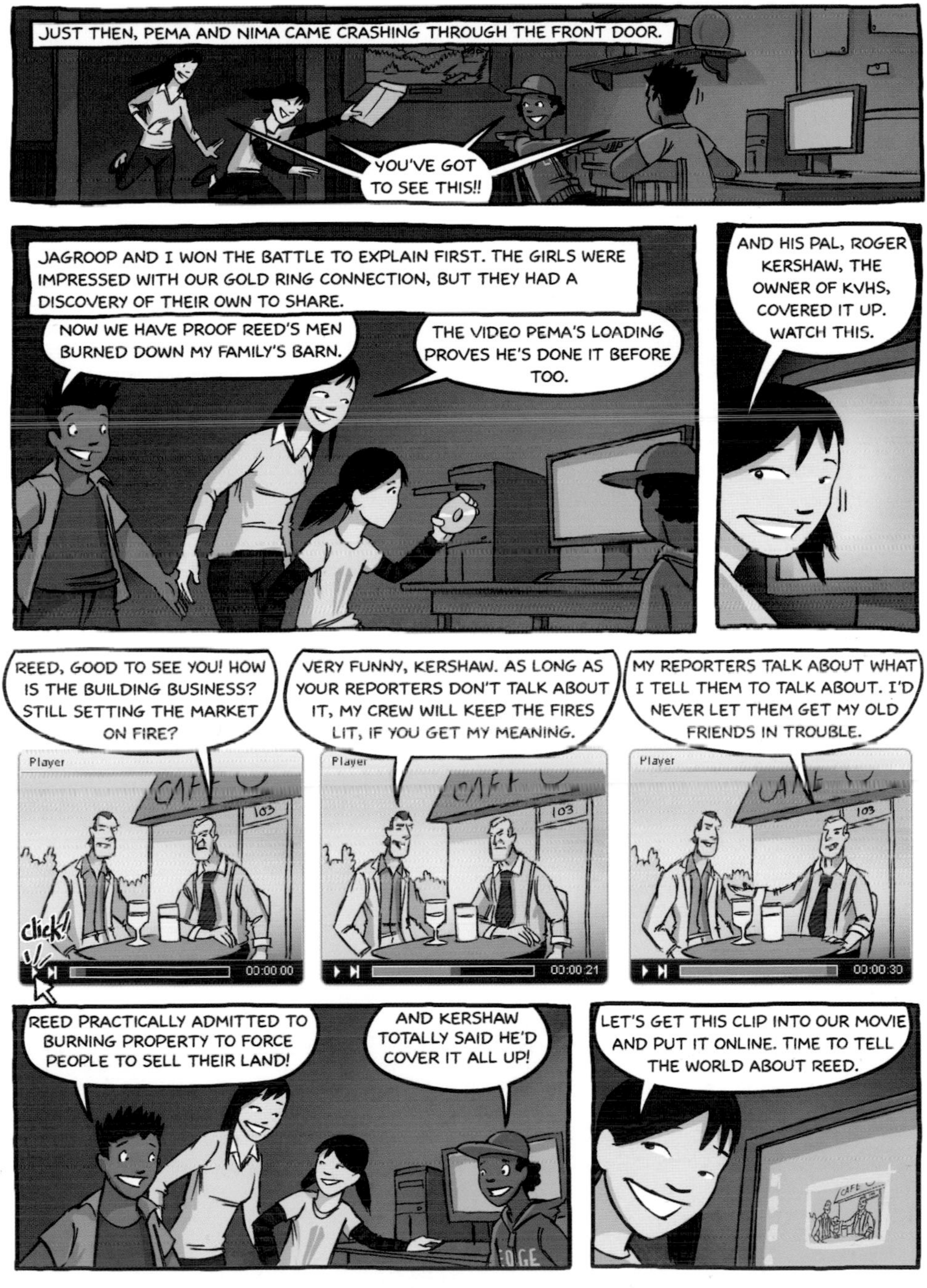
JUST THEN, PEMA AND NIMA CAME CRASHING THROUGH THE FRONT DOOR.
YOU'VE GOT TO SEE THIS!!
JAGROOP AND I WON THE BATTLE TO EXPLAIN FIRST. THE GIRLS WERE IMPRESSED WITH OUR GOLD RING CONNECTION, BUT THEY HAD A DISCOVERY OF THEIR OWN TO SHARE.
NOW WE HAVE PROOF REED'S MEN BURNED DOWN MY FAMILY'S BARN.
THE VIDEO PEMA'S LOADING PROVES HE'S DONE IT BEFORE TOO.
AND HIS PAL, ROGER KERSHAW, THE OWNER OF KVHS, COVERED IT UP. WATCH THIS.
REED, GOOD TO SEE YOU! HOW IS THE BUILDING BUSINESS? STILL SETTING THE MARKET ON FIRE?
Player
CAFE
103
Click!
00:00:00
VERY FUNNY, KERSHAW. AS LONG AS YOUR REPORTERS DON'T TALK ABOUT IT, MY CREW WILL KEEP THE FIRES LIT, IF YOU GET MY MEANING.
Player
103
00:00:21
MY REPORTERS TALK ABOUT WHAT I TELL THEM TO TALK ABOUT. I'D NEVER LET THEM GET MY OLD FRIENDS IN TROUBLE.
Player
103
00:00:30
REED PRACTICALLY ADMITTED TO BURNING PROPERTY TO FORCE PEOPLE TO SELL THEIR LAND!
AND KERSHAW TOTALLY SAID HE'D COVER IT ALL UP!
LET'S GET THIS CLIP INTO OUR MOVIE AND PUT IT ONLINE. TIME TO TELL THE WORLD ABOUT REED.

CHAPTER 6
WEATHERGIRL REBELLION

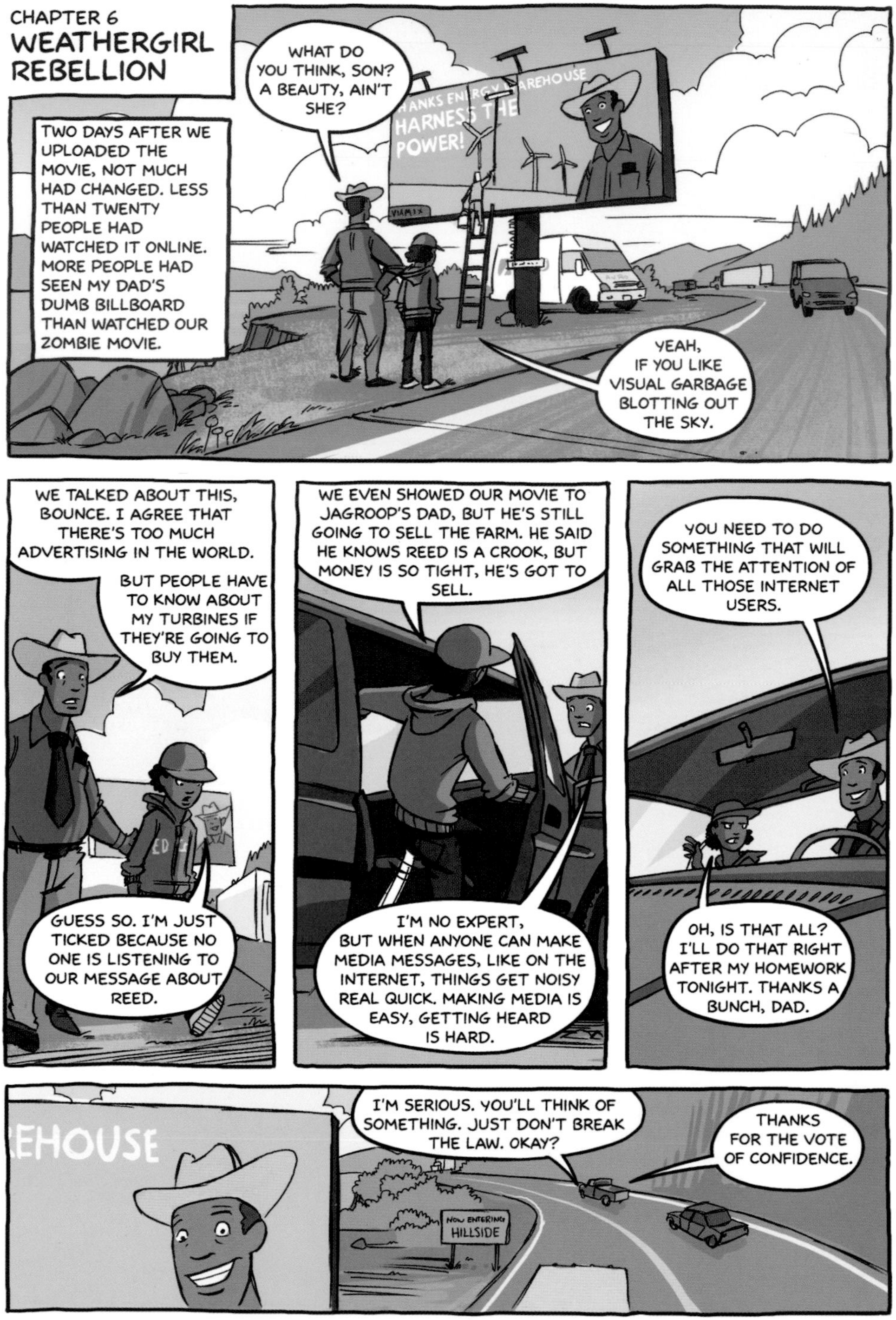
TWO DAYS AFTER WE UPLOADED THE MOVIE, NOT MUCH HAD CHANGED. LESS THAN TWENTY PEOPLE HAD WATCHED IT ONLINE. MORE PEOPLE HAD SEEN MY DAD'S DUMB BILLBOARD THAN WATCHED OUR ZOMBIE MOVIE.
WHAT DO YOU THINK, SON? A BEAUTY, AIN'T SHE?
HARNESS THE POWER!
YEAH, IF YOU LIKE VISUAL GARBAGE BLOTTING OUT THE SKY.
WE TALKED ABOUT THIS, BOUNCE. I AGREE THAT THERE'S TOO MUCH ADVERTISING IN THE WORLD.
BUT PEOPLE HAVE TO KNOW ABOUT MY TURBINES IF THEY'RE GOING TO BUY THEM.
GUESS SO. I'M JUST TICKED BECAUSE NO ONE IS LISTENING TO OUR MESSAGE ABOUT REED.
WE EVEN SHOWED OUR MOVIE TO JAGROOP'S DAD, BUT HE'S STILL GOING TO SELL THE FARM. HE SAID HE KNOWS REED IS A CROOK, BUT MONEY IS SO TIGHT, HE'S GOT TO SELL.
I'M NO EXPERT, BUT WHEN ANYONE CAN MAKE MEDIA MESSAGES, LIKE ON THE INTERNET, THINGS GET NOISY REAL QUICK. MAKING MEDIA IS EASY, GETTING HEARD IS HARD.
YOU NEED TO DO SOMETHING THAT WILL GRAB THE ATTENTION OF ALL THOSE INTERNET USERS.
OH, IS THAT ALL? I'LL DO THAT RIGHT AFTER MY HOMEWORK TONIGHT. THANKS A BUNCH, DAD.
I'M SERIOUS. YOU'LL THINK OF SOMETHING. JUST DON'T BREAK THE LAW. OKAY?
THANKS FOR THE VOTE OF CONFIDENCE.
NOW ENTERING HILLSIDE

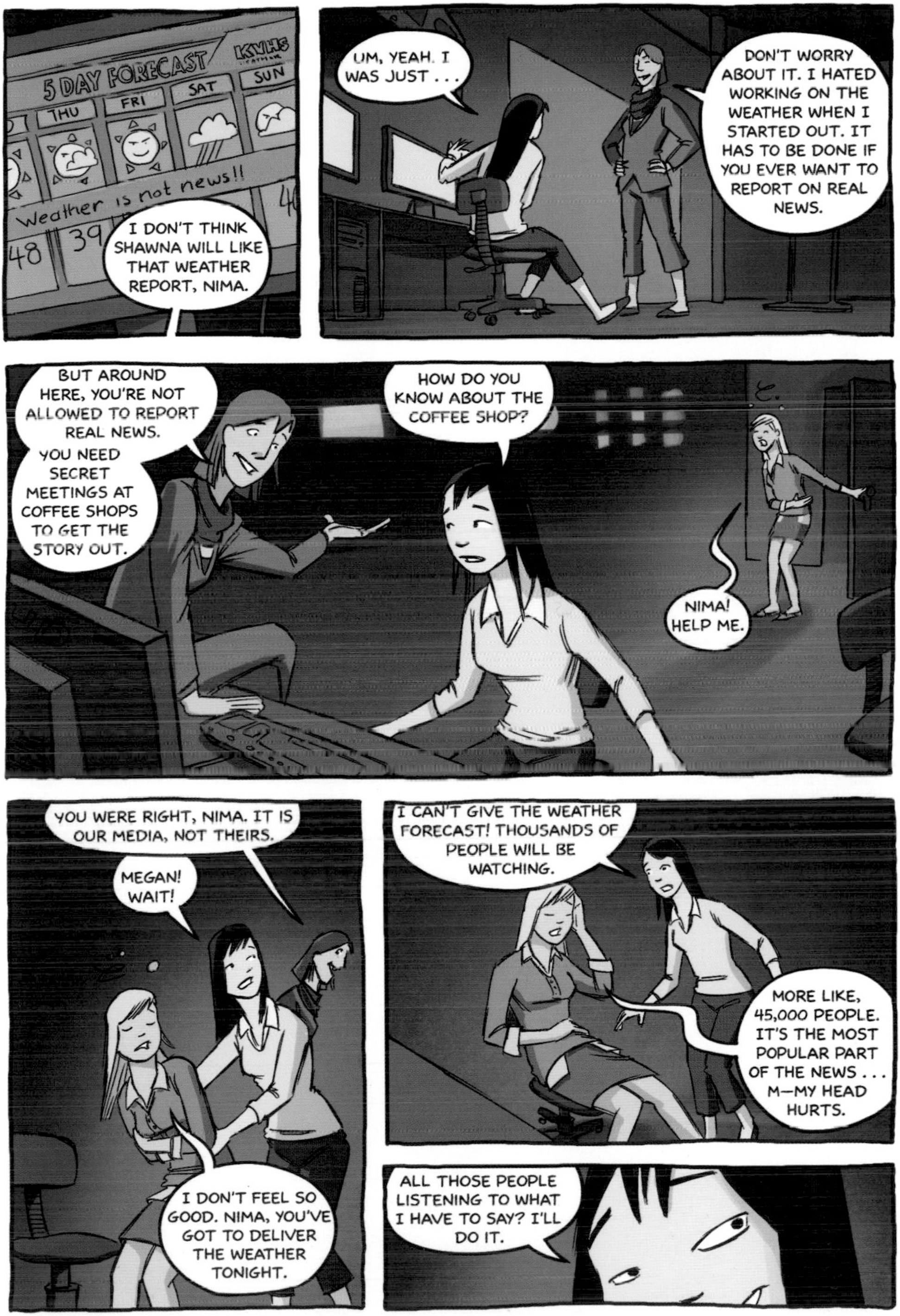
5 DAY FORECAST
KVHS
THU
FRI
SAT
SUN
Weather is not news!!
48
39
I DON'T THINK SHAWNA WILL LIKE THAT WEATHER REPORT, NIMA.
UM, YEAH. I WAS JUST . . .
DON'T WORRY ABOUT IT. I HATED WORKING ON THE WEATHER WHEN I STARTED OUT. IT HAS TO BE DONE IF YOU EVER WANT TO REPORT ON REAL NEWS.
BUT AROUND HERE, YOU'RE NOT ALLOWED TO REPORT REAL NEWS.
YOU NEED SECRET MEETINGS AT COFFEE SHOPS TO GET THE STORY OUT.
HOW DO YOU KNOW ABOUT THE COFFEE SHOP?
NIMA! HELP ME.
YOU WERE RIGHT, NIMA. IT IS OUR MEDIA, NOT THEIRS.
MEGAN! WAIT!
I DON'T FEEL SO GOOD. NIMA, YOU'VE GOT TO DELIVER THE WEATHER TONIGHT.
I CAN'T GIVE THE WEATHER FORECAST! THOUSANDS OF PEOPLE WILL BE WATCHING.
MORE LIKE, 45,000 PEOPLE. IT'S THE MOST POPULAR PART OF THE NEWS . . . M—MY HEAD HURTS.
ALL THOSE PEOPLE LISTENING TO WHAT I HAVE TO SAY? I'LL DO IT.

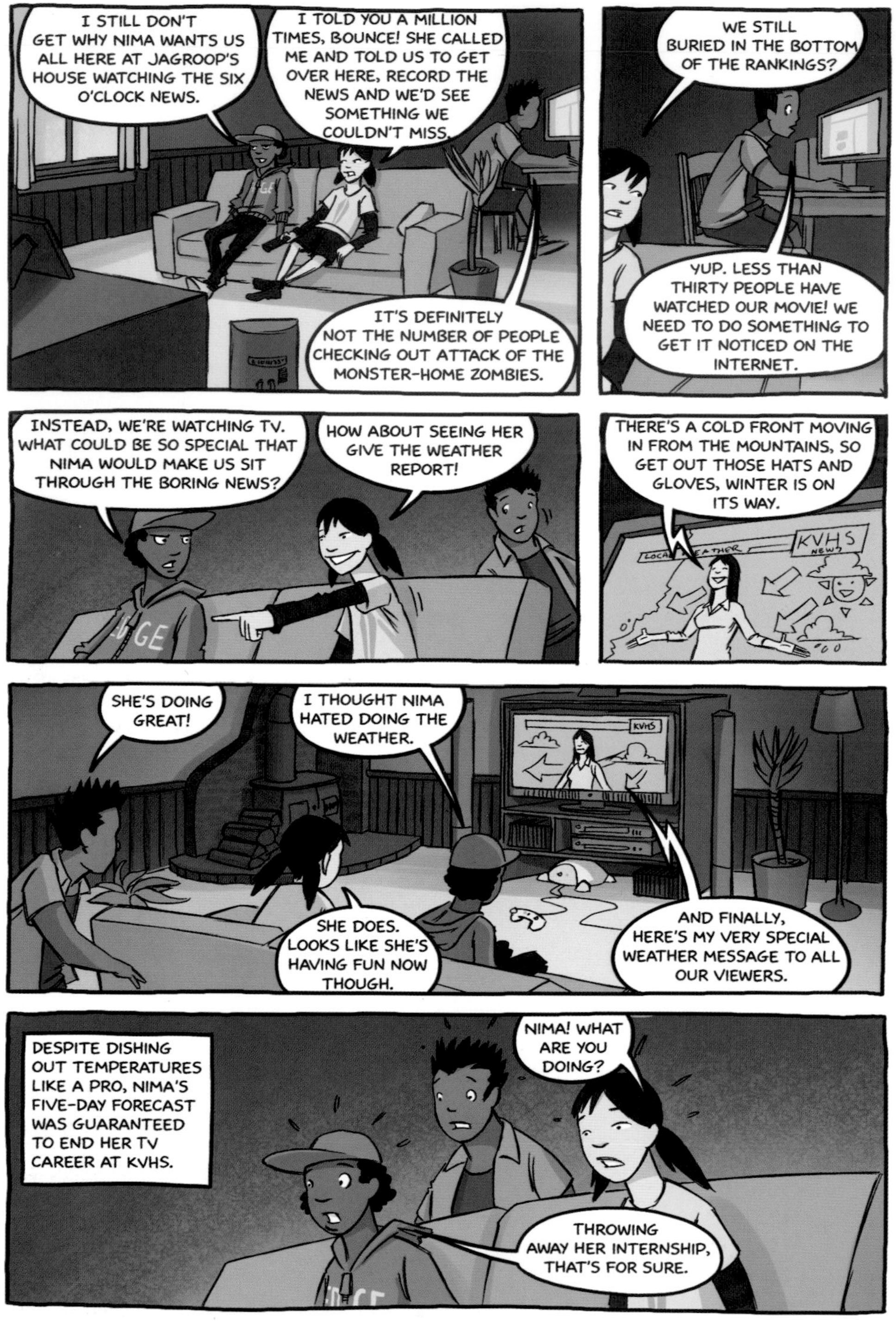
I STILL DON'T GET WHY NIMA WANTS US ALL HERE AT JAGROOP'S HOUSE WATCHING THE SIX O'CLOCK NEWS.
I TOLD YOU A MILLION TIMES, BOUNCE! SHE CALLED ME AND TOLD US TO GET OVER HERE, RECORD THE NEWS AND WE'D SEE SOMETHING WE COULDN'T MISS.
IT'S DEFINITELY NOT THE NUMBER OF PEOPLE CHECKING OUT ATTACK OF THE MONSTER-HOME ZOMBIES.
WE STILL BURIED IN THE BOTTOM OF THE RANKINGS?
YUP. LESS THAN THIRTY PEOPLE HAVE WATCHED OUR MOVIE! WE NEED TO DO SOMETHING TO GET IT NOTICED ON THE INTERNET.
INSTEAD, WE'RE WATCHING TV. WHAT COULD BE SO SPECIAL THAT NIMA WOULD MAKE US SIT THROUGH THE BORING NEWS?
HOW ABOUT SEEING HER GIVE THE WEATHER REPORT!
THERE'S A COLD FRONT MOVING IN FROM THE MOUNTAINS, SO GET OUT THOSE HATS AND GLOVES, WINTER IS ON ITS WAY.
KVHS
SHE'S DOING GREAT!
I THOUGHT NIMA HATED DOING THE WEATHER.
SHE DOES. LOOKS LIKE SHE'S HAVING FUN NOW THOUGH.
AND FINALLY, HERE'S MY VERY SPECIAL WEATHER MESSAGE TO ALL OUR VIEWERS.
DESPITE DISHING OUT TEMPERATURES LIKE A PRO, NIMA'S FIVE-DAY FORECAST WAS GUARANTEED TO END HER TV CAREER AT KVHS.
NIMA! WHAT ARE YOU DOING?
THROWING AWAY HER INTERNSHIP, THAT'S FOR SURE.

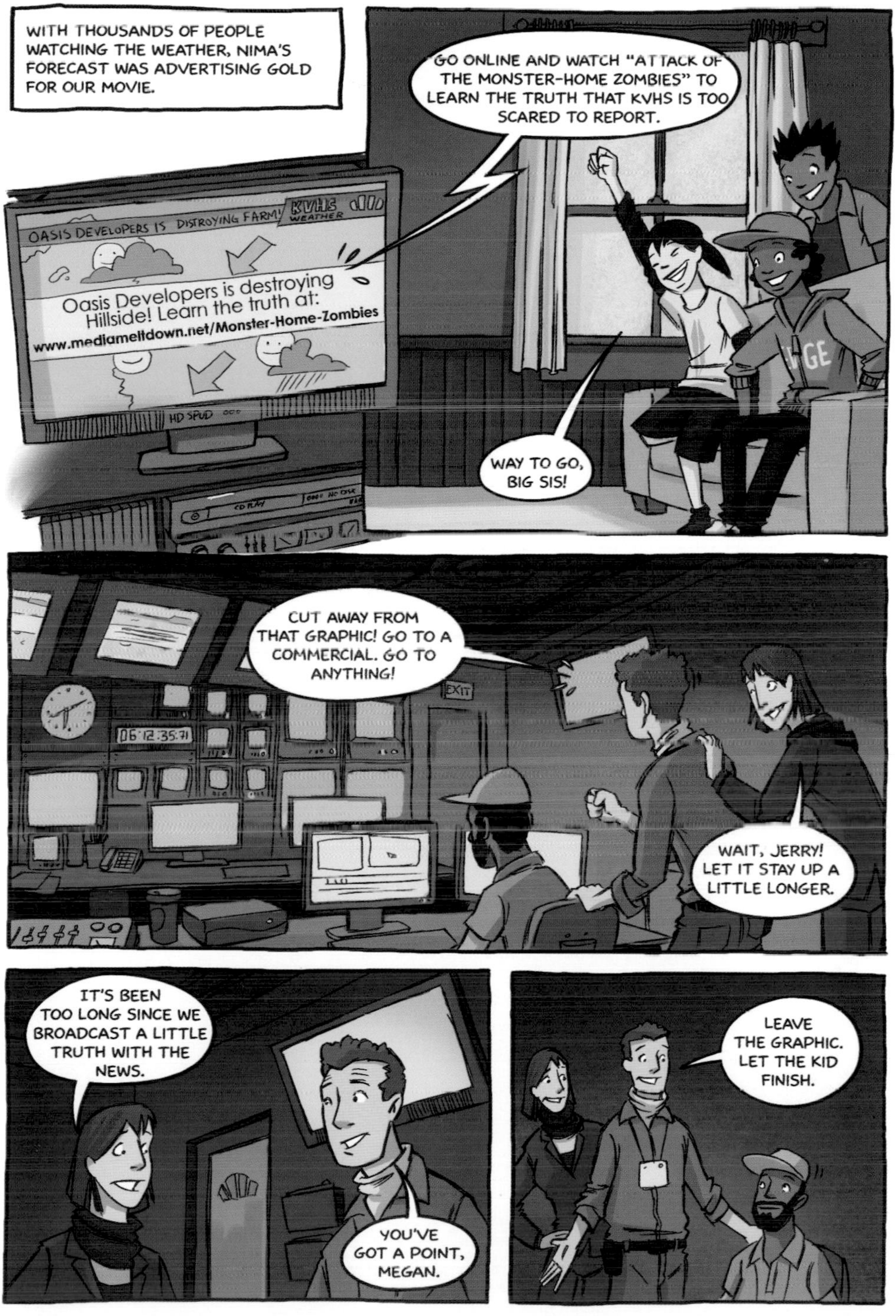
WITH THOUSANDS OF PEOPLE WATCHING THE WEATHER, NIMA'S FORECAST WAS ADVERTISING GOLD FOR OUR MOVIE.
KVHS WEATHER
OASIS DEVELOPERS IS DISTROYING FARM!
Oasis Developers is destroying Hillside! Learn the truth at:
www.mediameltdown.net/Monster-Home-Zombies
HD SPUD
GO ONLINE AND WATCH "ATTACK OF THE MONSTER-HOME ZOMBIES" TO LEARN THE TRUTH THAT KVHS IS TOO SCARED TO REPORT.
WAY TO GO, BIG SIS!
CUT AWAY FROM THAT GRAPHIC! GO TO A COMMERCIAL. GO TO ANYTHING!
EXIT
06:12:35:71
WAIT, JERRY! LET IT STAY UP A LITTLE LONGER.
IT'S BEEN TOO LONG SINCE WE BROADCAST A LITTLE TRUTH WITH THE NEWS.
YOU'VE GOT A POINT, MEGAN.
LEAVE THE GRAPHIC. LET THE KID FINISH.

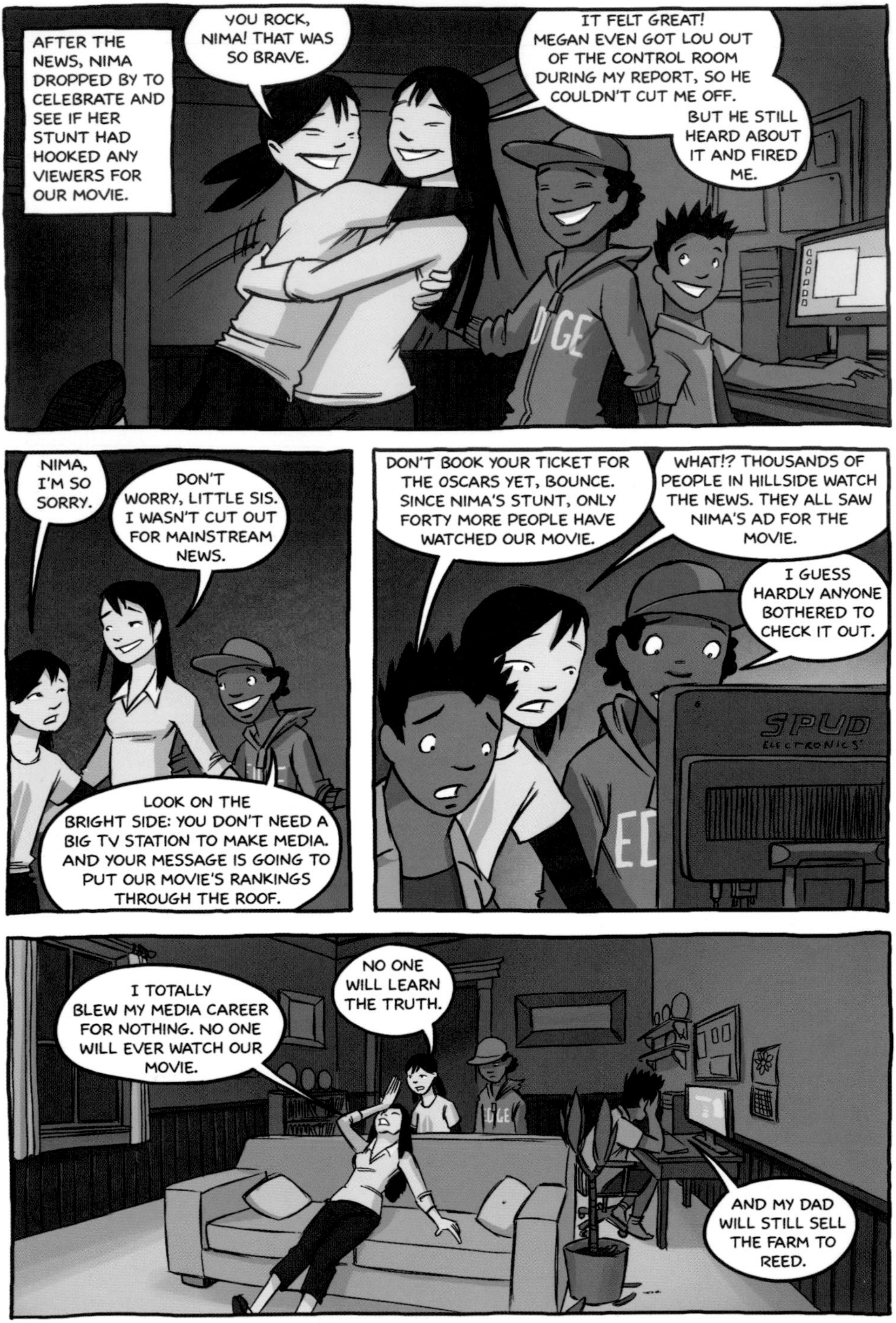
AFTER THE NEWS, NIMA DROPPED BY TO CELEBRATE AND SEE IF HER STUNT HAD HOOKED ANY VIEWERS FOR OUR MOVIE.
YOU ROCK, NIMA! THAT WAS SO BRAVE.
IT FELT GREAT! MEGAN EVEN GOT LOU OUT OF THE CONTROL ROOM DURING MY REPORT, SO HE COULDN'T CUT ME OFF.
BUT HE STILL HEARD ABOUT IT AND FIRED ME.
NIMA, I'M SO SORRY.
DON'T WORRY, LITTLE SIS. I WASN'T CUT OUT FOR MAINSTREAM NEWS.
LOOK ON THE BRIGHT SIDE: YOU DON'T NEED A BIG TV STATION TO MAKE MEDIA. AND YOUR MESSAGE IS GOING TO PUT OUR MOVIE'S RANKINGS THROUGH THE ROOF.
DON'T BOOK YOUR TICKET FOR THE OSCARS YET, BOUNCE. SINCE NIMA'S STUNT, ONLY FORTY MORE PEOPLE HAVE WATCHED OUR MOVIE.
WHAT!? THOUSANDS OF PEOPLE IN HILLSIDE WATCH THE NEWS. THEY ALL SAW NIMA'S AD FOR THE MOVIE.
I GUESS HARDLY ANYONE BOTHERED TO CHECK IT OUT.
SPUD ELECTRONICS
I TOTALLY BLEW MY MEDIA CAREER FOR NOTHING. NO ONE WILL EVER WATCH OUR MOVIE.
NO ONE WILL LEARN THE TRUTH.
AND MY DAD WILL STILL SELL THE FARM TO REED.

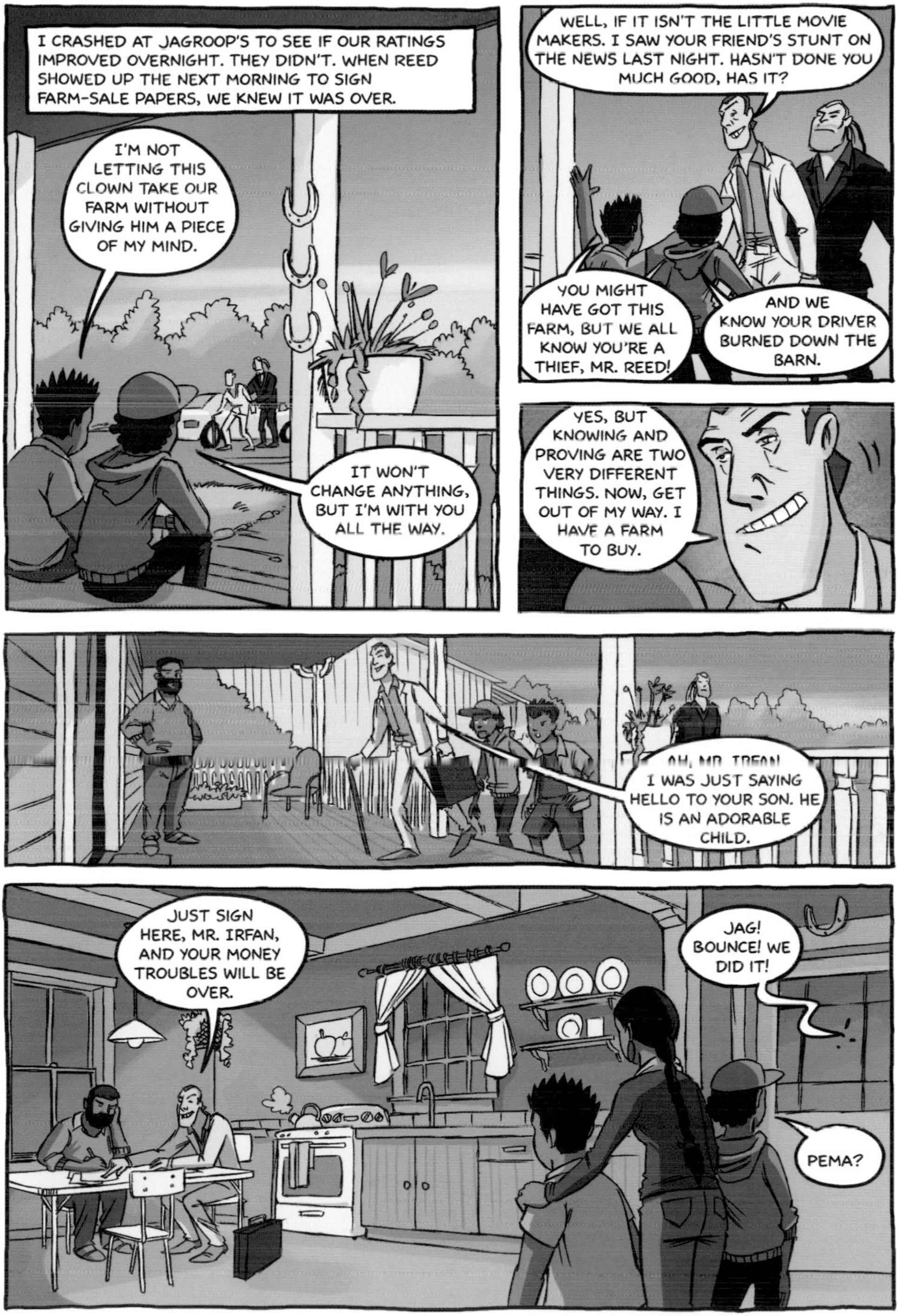
I CRASHED AT JAGROOP'S TO SEE IF OUR RATINGS IMPROVED OVERNIGHT. THEY DIDN'T. WHEN REED SHOWED UP THE NEXT MORNING TO SIGN FARM-SALE PAPERS, WE KNEW IT WAS OVER.
I'M NOT LETTING THIS CLOWN TAKE OUR FARM WITHOUT GIVING HIM A PIECE OF MY MIND.
IT WON'T CHANGE ANYTHING, BUT I'M WITH YOU ALL THE WAY.
WELL, IF IT ISN'T THE LITTLE MOVIE MAKERS. I SAW YOUR FRIEND'S STUNT ON THE NEWS LAST NIGHT. HASN'T DONE YOU MUCH GOOD, HAS IT?
YOU MIGHT HAVE GOT THIS FARM, BUT WE ALL KNOW YOU'RE A THIEF, MR. REED!
AND WE KNOW YOUR DRIVER BURNED DOWN THE BARN.
YES, BUT KNOWING AND PROVING ARE TWO VERY DIFFERENT THINGS. NOW, GET OUT OF MY WAY. I HAVE A FARM TO BUY.
AH, MR. IRFAN!
I WAS JUST SAYING HELLO TO YOUR SON. HE IS AN ADORABLE CHILD.
JUST SIGN HERE, MR. IRFAN, AND YOUR MONEY TROUBLES WILL BE OVER.
JAG! BOUNCE! WE DID IT!
PEMA?

PEMA, NIMA, WHAT ARE YOU DOING HERE?

WE'VE BEEN BOINGBOINGED!

OUR MOVIE IS A HIT! OVER 100,000 PEOPLE HAVE WATCHED IT! THANKS TO NIMA'S WEATHER STUNT LAST NIGHT, WE'RE ALL OVER THE WEB.

boingboing
A DIRECTORY OF WONDERFUL THINGS

Teen Intern Hijacks Weather to Expose Land Developer
POSTED BY ISLANDGIRL · OCTOBER 10, 2009 10:17 PM | PERMALINK

LOCAL WEATHER · KVHS

SALE 10% off CLICK HERE

Media intern, Nima Chan, takes over KVHS news to tell the truth about crooked land developer, Karl Reed. His company, Oasis Developers, has been intimidating farmers to sell their land . . .

SOMEONE UPLOADED NIMA'S WEATHER REPORT AND SENT IT TO BOINGBOING.NET.

THAT SITE ROCKS! MILLIONS OF PEOPLE VISIT IT EVERY DAY.

MILLIONS OF PEOPLE WHO WILL LEARN THE TRUTH ABOUT REED.

ALREADY OVER 100,000 PEOPLE HAVE WATCHED OUR MOVIE. MORE ARE CHECKING IT OUT EVERY MINUTE!

AND A BUNCH OF BLOGGERS HAVE DUG UP MORE DIRT ON REED AND SENT IT TO THE COPS.

THE "BURN DOWN THE BARN TO SCARE THE FARMERS" TRICK IS ONE OF REED'S FAVORITES. HE'S DONE IT IN THREE OTHER TOWNS ACROSS THE COUNTRY.

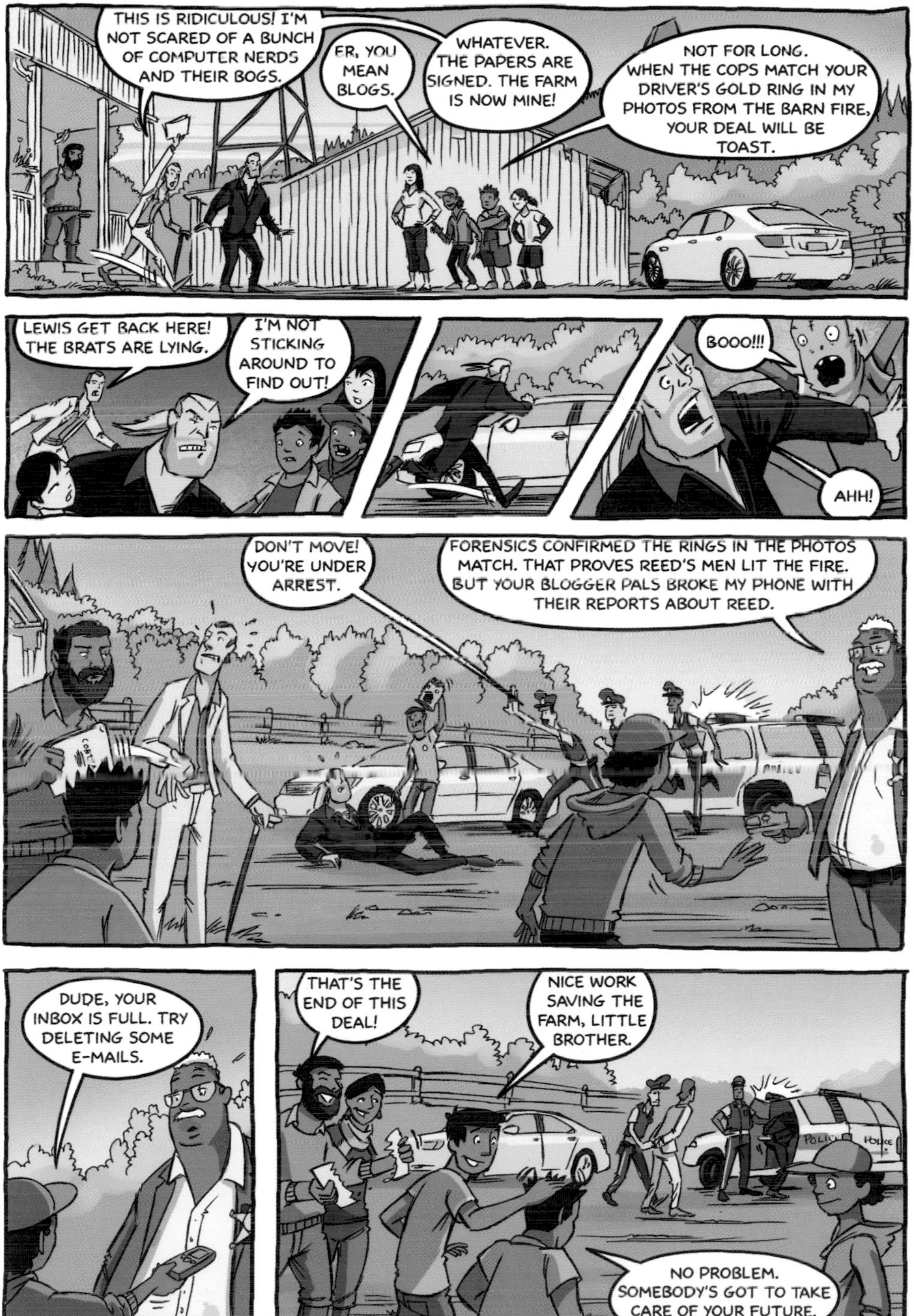
THIS IS RIDICULOUS! I'M NOT SCARED OF A BUNCH OF COMPUTER NERDS AND THEIR BOGS.
ER, YOU MEAN BLOGS.
WHATEVER. THE PAPERS ARE SIGNED. THE FARM IS NOW MINE!
NOT FOR LONG. WHEN THE COPS MATCH YOUR DRIVER'S GOLD RING IN MY PHOTOS FROM THE BARN FIRE, YOUR DEAL WILL BE TOAST.
LEWIS GET BACK HERE! THE BRATS ARE LYING.
I'M NOT STICKING AROUND TO FIND OUT!
BOOO!!!
AHH!
DON'T MOVE! YOU'RE UNDER ARREST.
FORENSICS CONFIRMED THE RINGS IN THE PHOTOS MATCH. THAT PROVES REED'S MEN LIT THE FIRE. BUT YOUR BLOGGER PALS BROKE MY PHONE WITH THEIR REPORTS ABOUT REED.
DUDE, YOUR INBOX IS FULL. TRY DELETING SOME E-MAILS.
THAT'S THE END OF THIS DEAL!
NICE WORK SAVING THE FARM, LITTLE BROTHER.
NO PROBLEM. SOMEBODY'S GOT TO TAKE CARE OF YOUR FUTURE.

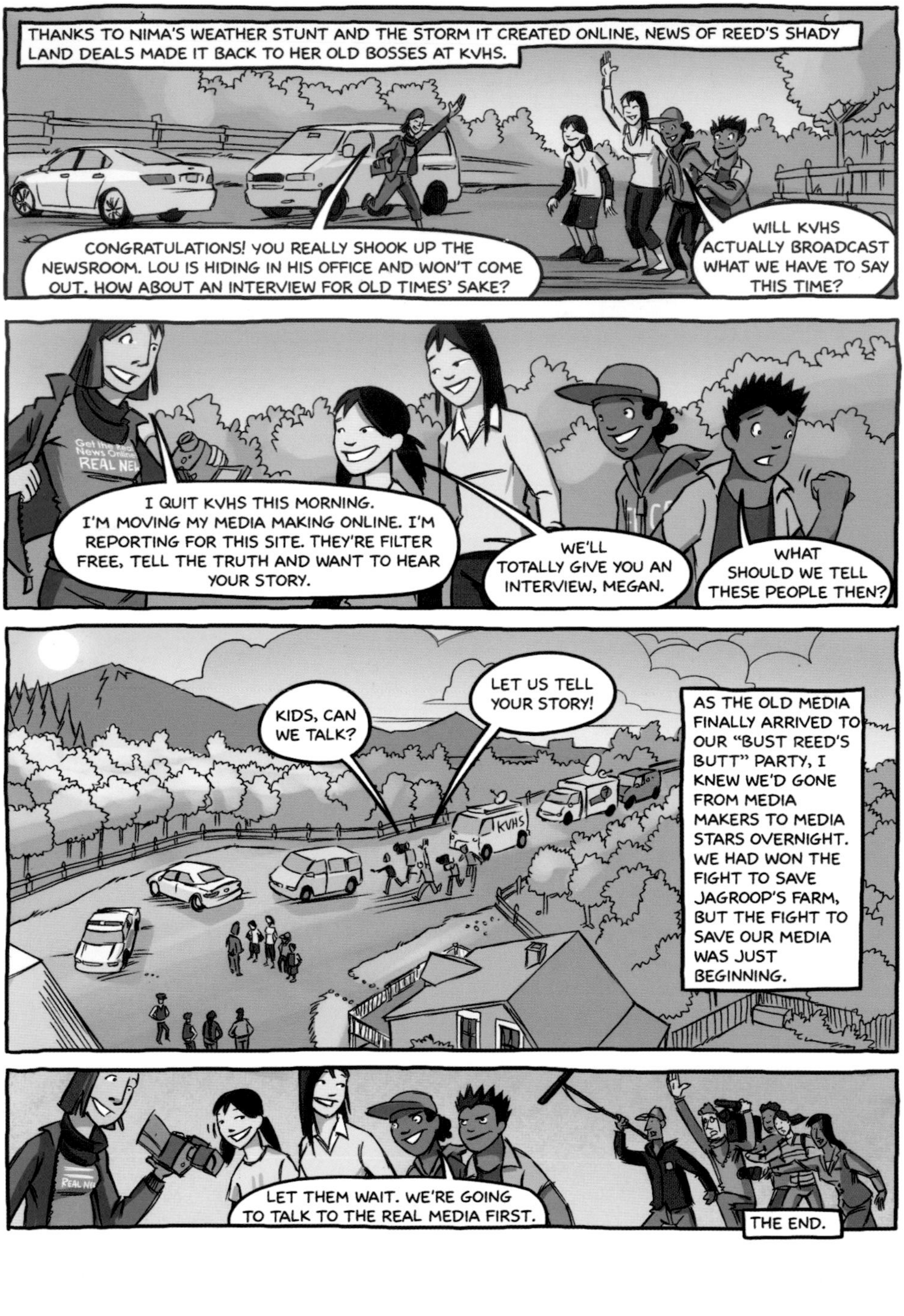
THANKS TO NIMA'S WEATHER STUNT AND THE STORM IT CREATED ONLINE, NEWS OF REED'S SHADY LAND DEALS MADE IT BACK TO HER OLD BOSSES AT KVHS.
CONGRATULATIONS! YOU REALLY SHOOK UP THE NEWSROOM. LOU IS HIDING IN HIS OFFICE AND WON'T COME OUT. HOW ABOUT AN INTERVIEW FOR OLD TIMES' SAKE?
WILL KVHS ACTUALLY BROADCAST WHAT WE HAVE TO SAY THIS TIME?
I QUIT KVHS THIS MORNING. I'M MOVING MY MEDIA MAKING ONLINE. I'M REPORTING FOR THIS SITE. THEY'RE FILTER FREE, TELL THE TRUTH AND WANT TO HEAR YOUR STORY.
WE'LL TOTALLY GIVE YOU AN INTERVIEW, MEGAN.
WHAT SHOULD WE TELL THESE PEOPLE THEN?
KIDS, CAN WE TALK?
LET US TELL YOUR STORY!
KVHS
AS THE OLD MEDIA FINALLY ARRIVED TO OUR "BUST REED'S BUTT" PARTY, I KNEW WE'D GONE FROM MEDIA MAKERS TO MEDIA STARS OVERNIGHT. WE HAD WON THE FIGHT TO SAVE JAGROOP'S FARM, BUT THE FIGHT TO SAVE OUR MEDIA WAS JUST BEGINNING.
LET THEM WAIT. WE'RE GOING TO TALK TO THE REAL MEDIA FIRST.
THE END.